James VanOosting
THE LAST PAYBACK

HarperCollins*Publishers*

Library of Congress Cataloging-in-Publication Data
VanOosting, James.
    The last payback / James VanOosting.
        p.   cm.
    Summary: Getting revenge for the death of her twin brother will be
hard for sixth-grader Dimple Dorfman, expecially because she thinks
that he was shot by the boy she likes best in her small town.
    ISBN 0-06-027491-3. — ISBN 0-06-027492-1 (lib. bdg.)
    [1. Death—Fiction.   2. Twins—Fiction.]   I. Title.
PZ7.V3425Las   1997
[Fic]—dc20   96-41300
                                                                                 CIP
                                                                                  AC

Typography by Steve Scott
1   2   3   4   5   6   7   8   9   10

First Edition

Kiss me, my sisters and my brother
For Kathi, Peg, and Jeff

THE LAST PAYBACK

CHAPTER ONE

Nobody would tell me what happened to him. Not Mama. Not Daddy. Not even Ivy June, my worst friend, who happens to blab for an occupation. They only went, "He got hurt." Just like that and nothing more. All except for Ivy June, who had to go and add "bad."

It's plain mean in my book not to tell a girl when her brother's died. And if they're twins, like him and me are, then it's worse. Then it's a sin. I don't care if you mean well, you're worried about my feelings, or what. That doesn't matter. It's still a sin.

And stupid, also. What did they think? Like I wasn't gonna notice? Hah.

Of course, Ivy June wasn't blessed with a brain, as everybody knows. But I'd of thought Mama and Daddy might have one, between 'em.

When they finally do get around to telling me the truth of it—'cause you can't keep a thing like that secret forever—I . . . am . . . angry, believe me. I will not forgive 'em. Not one of 'em. Not Mama, not Daddy, not Ivy June—for sure not Ivy June—

so long as I live, so help me God. Even if that means I'm going to hell, which is a place I know to exist.

Dale was my brother, Dale *is* my brother, and I will not forgive 'em. Not now and not ever.

The night it happened, Saturday, he went over to play at Ronnie's. The *Cuthbur Examiner* might not want to print his name, but I don't mind who knows. Why should I? I'll give it to you straight out. Ronnie Delaney. That's him! Who cares if he was the first boy that kissed me? Who cares if I was planning on marrying him? It would be a sacrilege to forgive Ronnie now. Dale wouldn't do it, you better believe. If it had been me died, Dale would probably march right over there and shoot Ronnie Delaney. *Ka-blooey*, that's what Dale would do.

Now they admit it, of course. Now, when it's too late and he's gone, they confess how I said he shouldn't of gone over there to Ronnie's. Mama says she can recall *now* how I had this, like, premonition. Right there at the supper table, with her serving us one of her smoky-link pizzas, I'm like, "Why do you gotta go over to Ronnie's tonight, huh?"

And Dale's like, "Nothing to do here."

And I go, "Is, too. *I* got plenty to do right here."

And he goes, "Like what?"

And I go, "Better stuff than you got over there at Ronnie's."

And he goes, "Nuh-uh," which is as good as agreeing with me, in my book.

But do you think somebody's gonna listen to a girl? In the sixth grade? Name of Dimple? Oh sure, right. Hah.

When I was a baby, they called me Dimples. Plural. Then somewhere along the line I chubbed up and lost one of 'em. So I changed my name myself to just plain Dimple. I'm very big on details, that's one thing about me. I cannot agree when Daddy says it's the thought what counts.

If that's true, then Dale would still be alive.

You tell me, is he? Well?

Detail is my middle name. Dimple Detail Dorfman.

My brother's middle name is more like Careless. Or Carefree. Something like that. Dale Carefree Dorfman.

Not anymore, it isn't.

The call didn't come from Mr. or Mrs. Delaney, oh no. It come straight from the cops, so right there you know something's wrong.

Mama picks up and goes, "Oh my gawd," just like in the movies when somebody gets bumped off by surprise. "Oh my gawd," she goes. Then she covers the mouthpiece and mouths at us, "It's the po-lice."

Which perks Daddy right up, who's been lying on the sofa snoozing in front of the Bulls' game. "What's wrong?" he goes. "What's wrong?"

Mama's listening hard, trying to catch all the details.

Daddy keeps going, "What's wrong? What happened?" with him looking at me like I'm the one who went, "Oh my gawd."

I just shrug.

Mama hangs up and is like, "Dale's hurt, Marvin. We gotta get down to the hospital."

So Daddy rouses himself, hoisting up on one elbow, and swings his legs over the edge, landing both feet on the floor. It's the end of the third quarter with the Bulls playing the Knicks nip-and-tuck. "What do you mean 'hurt'?" he wants to know.

Mama goes, "Just hurt, okay? Shake a leg."

Seems nobody wants to notice me standing there. Maybe I've turned invisible or something. Real loud, I say, "I'm coming too."

And Mama's like, "No, Dimple, you stay here."

"But Dale's hurt."

"You'll only be in the way," Daddy goes, patting

4

me on the head while he switches off the game.

"I won't be in anybody's way."

"Hush now," Mama goes.

I ask 'em, "What happened to Dale?"

"Get a move on, Marvin."

"How come the cops called?" I wanta know.

"Just a precaution," Mama goes, which doesn't even begin to answer my question.

So then I start shouting at 'em, trying to call attention. "He's my brother! Dale is my brother!" This is an important point, I believe.

"You stay put right here, Dimple," Daddy goes, "and I'll call you up from the hospital. How's that?"

I'm thinking, "No good," but I don't say this out loud.

Mama's like, "Did you hear your daddy, Dimple? We're gonna call you up, okay?"

I try to refresh their memory about how things are. I go, real slow, "He . . . is . . . my . . . twin . . . brother."

And Mama's like, "That's right, honey, so you need to stay here at home. Won't be no use your going down to the hospital and witnessing what none of us wants to see."

Both of them are putting on their jackets. Daddy is wearing his shiny Bulls one me and

5

Dale bought him last Christmas. I know there's no use in arguing.

"Just tell me what happened to him, will you?" I go, hearing the whine in my own voice now.

"Be a big girl," Mama says, "and try not to worry none. Soon as we know what's happening, we'll call you up on the telephone. Okay?"

I don't go "uh-huh," to give her any satisfaction, but just nod so she won't repeat it again.

And then they leave out the front door, revving up the motor of our Malibu Classic, with Daddy backfiring it from overexcitement.

I kick around the house, turn the Bulls game back on, sit down and watch somebody miss a three-pointer, and then go out to see if there's any more Pringles in the kitchen. There is.

I'm way too hepped up to sit still and watch any basketball—even *if* the Knicks and us are tied for best record in the East—but I don't got anything else to do either. So the idea pops into my head to call up Ivy June. She lives right next door to the Delaneys. Maybe she knows what's happening.

"Ivy June?" I go.

She's like, "Yes?"—all stuck up and proper.

"This is Dimple."

She doesn't answer.

"You know, Dimple Dorfman."

"Yes, I know who you are."

"Have you been there at your house all night?" I go.

"Yes."

I'm trying to sound casual, so I don't give her any advantage. This is very hard to do when talking with Ivy June. "Say, did you happen to see my brother over there at Ronnie's?"

"Of course I did, Dimple. Everybody knows."

"Knows what?"

"Knows what happened."

"Well, I don't, Ivy June. I don't know what happened."

"You don't?" she goes, sounding all fancy and fussy, making like my ignorance is some kinda crime.

I bite my tongue, trying to stay polite as I can. "No. All I know is the police called, and Mama and Daddy had to go down to the hospital."

"What did they tell you?" she goes.

"They went, 'Dale's hurt,' that's all."

"Nothing else?"

"No, you ditz."

"Watch your tongue, Dimple Dorfman. Do you know who you're talking to?"

"Yes, I do," I go, "and you better tell me what

happened to my brother real quick, or I'm coming right over there and pulling a handful of your hair clean outta your head."

That does the trick. Ivy June opposes pain.

"Okay, all right," she goes. "But don't you come over here, Dimple, or my mother will not let you in this house."

"You better tell me then," I warn her, "because I'm not so stupid as to come in by your front door, girl. Not if I really want to get you. There's more than one way to skin a cat, you know."

I can hear how scared she is now from the sound of her voice.

"I'll tell you. I'll tell you," she goes. "But you got to promise not to come over here."

"Tell me first."

Out of my left eye I see how the Bulls are giving away their lead, letting the Knicks muscle 'em out of the lane for rebounds.

"Okay," she goes, "but you got to keep your promise."

"I'm waiting, Ivy June. Start talking."

On the offensive end, they pull down a board right over the back of our center, and the refs don't call a foul. It's as plain as the nose on their face, but no call. Sheez.

"All I know," Ivy June goes, "is what I could see

8

from the window of our parlor."

"What did you see?"

"I could see them taking him out on a stretcher through the Delaneys' front door to the ambulance."

"There was a *ambulance*? They took Dale in a *ambulance*?"

"Of course they took him in an ambulance, Dimple. What did you expect? Your brother's hurt *bad*."

"How do you know he's hurt *bad*?"

"Why else would there be an ambulance? And, besides, that's what Mrs. Delaney said."

"You talked to Mrs. Delaney?"

"My mother did."

"And what did *she* say?"

Ivy June stops talking for a minute, so I gotta jump-start her up again. "What did Mrs. Delaney say?"

"I'm sorry, Dimple, but I can't tell you any more."

"What do you mean you can't tell me any more?"

"My mother says it's not right for us to be the ones telling you this."

"Telling me what?" I go, all exasperated. "You ain't told me a thing yet." I'm shouting into the mouthpiece now. "You tell me exactly what

9

happened to my brother right this minute, Ivy June, or else."

"Or else what?"

"Or else people are gonna be calling you 'skinhead,' girl, 'cause that's exactly how much hair you're gonna have left."

Then she starts whimpering. "That's not fair, Dimple Dorfman. My father will call the police if you so much as pull one hair out of my head."

"Well, if you want to keep your pretty hair, you better tell me about my brother, and I mean *now*."

"He's hurt bad, Dimple. That's all I can say. Don't make me tell you anything more."

Right now I'm madder at Ivy June than I ever was before, and that makes some kinda record. "You better dial 911, girl, because you're gonna need some po-lice pro-tection. You hear me?" And I hang up. Let her chew on that for a while.

The game's over, and I flip off the set without finding out who won.

I believe it is not right for one twin to get himself hurt real bad and for the other twin to be left ignorant. Not with the whole world knowing all about it. That's what I'm thinking. There oughta be a law against this. In fact, there *is* a law against this. It's called the law of nature. Mama and Daddy and Ivy June, every one of 'em, is breaking this law of nature.

I march back into the kitchen and yank the telephone book off the shelf to look up Cuthbur Deaconess. Down at the hospital they *got* to tell you what's happening, don't they? I punch in the numbers.

"Cuthbur Deaconess Hospital. How shall I direct your call?"

"Hello. My brother's there," I go, "and I wanta know how he's doing."

"What's the patient's name, ma'am?"

"His name's Dale, Dale Dorfman."

"One minute, please."

The voice on the other end of the line's got no attitude, and I'm grateful.

"Ma'am?" it says.

"What'd you find out?"

"I'm going to have to transfer you to the emergency room, okay? You just hold the line."

"Thank you."

At the sound of the words "emergency room," I get a funny feeling. Finally somebody knows where Dale is, and I'm gonna get some answers. That's the good part. But before I can put words to the bad thought, some man's voice breaks onto the line.

"Can I help you?" he asks. This one's got an attitude, I can tell, and it isn't the helpful kind.

"I wanta know how my brother's doing," I go. "His name is Dale Dorfman."

"And who are you?"

"Who am I?" Sheez. I gotta cop some patience, because this man holds all the cards. "I'm his sister. My name is Dimple Dorfman."

"And how old are you, Miss Dorfman?"

"I'm his *twin* sister."

There's a long silence while this wiseguy uses all his smarts to figure how old that makes me.

"I'm sorry, miss," he goes. "We can't give out that information to minors. You'll have to wait and speak to your parents."

"Hold on a minute. You don't understand something here," I go. "Him and me are twins. Whatever goes on with Dale goes on with me, and the other way around. See? You gotta tell me how he's doing."

"It's regulations, miss. There's nothing I can do."

"Whose regulations?" I ask him.

"The hospital's, miss."

Then I totally lose it. "Do you got any twins working down there at the hospital?"

"I don't see your point, miss."

"That's true, mister. You sure as hell don't," I holler at him before slamming down the receiver.

I'm pulling on my ski jacket—with this new thinsulation stuff keeps you warm without showing much bulk—when Daddy comes in the front door.

"Dale's dead, Dimple," he goes, too tuckered to beat around the bush.

"*What?*"

"Your brother's died, honey. I'm sorrier than—"

"*How?*" I shout.

Daddy goes, "Come here, sweetheart."

So I scootch inside his Bulls jacket and lean up against his hot chest. His heart is thumping a mile a minute under there.

"How could Dale die?" I ask him, pressing the words out hard, trying to piece together something that makes any kind of sense.

But Daddy doesn't speak again. Maybe he's crying, who knows.

I cannot believe this. It takes me till too late to find out *what* happened to my brother. Then nobody wants to tell me *how* it happened. Sheez. Who do they think I am, anyway?

CHAPTER TWO

When Mama comes home from the hospital, she's pooped and ticked all at the same time. Looks bad. She's standing droop-shouldered by the front door, so I get up off the sofa and go to her. As I'm walking across the parlor, I can picture how this scene would go in a movie: young girl comforts mother despite her own terrible heartbreak. I'm feeling genuine sorry for Mama but, at the same time, it feels so unreal. "Sorry, Mama," I say.

She hugs me to her, pressing my face against her chest. "Oh, Dimple," she groans, kinda wringing out my name. "I'm sorry too, sweetheart." She takes a big sniff, trying not to cry. "It shouldn't of happened, Dimple. He's gone, and it shouldn't of happened."

I pull out of her hug. "*What* shouldn't of happened?" I ask her. "Nobody will tell me anything except Dale's dead. I don't know how. I don't know why."

"Please, Dimple, I just can't talk about it now. Try to understand."

I know I should keep my mouth shut, but how am I supposed to do that when my twin brother has died and nobody's telling me the story? It's *my* story, too, for crying out loud.

Mama walks into the living room toward Daddy. "Dimple," she says, "you call up Ivy June now and apologize, honey, you hear?"

"Apologize? For what?"

"For saying you're gonna pull out all her hair, sweetheart. That wasn't nice."

Now, how'd she hear about that, I'd like to know? You don't think Ivy June's mother would call her up at the hospital to snitch, do you? I cannot believe this.

I stomp right past Mama and march up the stairs without finishing the scene the way I wanted to. Lucky for her she doesn't follow me. There's gonna be no apologies from Dimple Dorfman. No apologies. And no forgiveness. No way. Sheez.

I clump up to my bedroom, slam the door, and keep on turning the lock around and around, forgetting how it's busted. Then I remember, so I inch my dresser up against it for a barricade.

I plop down on my bed and feel the steam vaporizing out my eyeballs. If this was a dumb movie or a stupid kid's book, I'd be bawling my eyes out right now. "Boo-hoo, my brother's dead." But this is real life, and heck, you can't cry buckets of tears when your temperature's past the boiling point. I am steamed, brother.

After a while, Daddy comes knock-knocking at the door and calls in real quiet. "Dimple, honey?"

"What?"

He's like, "Don't be mad at your mama now. She's all upset. She can't help herself, what with seeing Dale that way and all."

"Why?" I go. "What does Dale look like?"

By this time, I'm laying flat on my bed and thinking, "What? Was Dale smashed up or something? Did he have his head busted in?"

Daddy's pushing at the door. "Let me in, Dimple."

"What's he look like?" I ask again.

"You know, honey."

"How would I know? Was I there?"

He keeps pushing against the door, and the dresser starts budging a little on my side. "Don't do this, Dimple," he goes.

"You stay out, you hear?"

"Come on, honey."

"I want to be alone, Daddy."

He doesn't answer right away. Probably he's thinking it over. "Okay, sweetheart, you be alone if that's what you want. But don't be mad at your mama, hear? She loves you, and I love you. We need to hang together now."

All I say is, "I'm not calling up Ivy June and apologizing. No way."

Daddy's like, "You don't have to."

It takes a second for his change of heart to sink in. Then I go, "Anyhow, you know I wasn't gonna pull out all her hair."

"I know that, honey." His voice sounds soft, like it can get sometimes.

"Just most of it."

He doesn't answer, and I appreciate that. Daddy's got some understanding now and again. Even so, until he tells me what happened, he's gotta stay on my list of Thou-Shalt-Not-Forgives.

Early Sunday morning, I begin to get a clearer picture of how things really are. The *Cuthbur Examiner* is throwed on our front stoop about six o'clock. Mama and Daddy don't figure me and Dale read it except for the funnies, but what do they know? How are you going to keep up on the Bulls' stats if you don't read the paper, huh? Sheez.

The headline says CUTHBUR YOUTH DIES IN SHOOTING, smack across the top, in big screamin' letters like the U. S. of A. just bombed somebody or something. I sit down on the sofa trying to hold my hands steady. Mama and Daddy are upstairs still, so I can settle in thoughtful.

17

A 12-year-old Cuthbur boy was accidentally killed Saturday night when a gun that he and a friend were playing with discharged.

Dale M. Dorfman of 153 N. Birch St. was pronounced dead on arrival at 9 P.M. at Cuthbur Deaconess Hospital.

He was struck in the chest by a .22-caliber bullet.

Sheriff McNally said it appears the victim and another youngster found the gun while playing Nintendo in a bedroom of the friend's house. The shooting occurred at 8:42 P.M.

"There were two kids in the room when the gun went off," McNally said. "We definitely feel it was an accident. There is nothing to indicate otherwise."

Police believe the loaded gun was found underneath a mattress in the bedroom.

Officials are not releasing the name of the other child who was with Dorfman. McNally also said he does not expect any charges to be filed.

An autopsy will be conducted.

The victim was a sixth-grade student at Cuthbur Elementary. He is survived by his parents, Marvin and Doris Dorfman, and

See BOY, 2A

18

I gotta search inside the paper to find the rest of it. Seems like the story of a boy getting shot ought to fit all on the front page. That's what I believe.

BOY KILLED IN SHOOTING
Continued from Page 1

by his twin sister, Dorothea.

Sheriff McNally emphasized that people need to "use common sense" if guns and children are in the house. "If you got children in the house, and a hunting weapon, or what-have-you, lock it up," McNally said. "They make trigger guards to where the gun won't fire without a key; there are steel storage cabinets.

"People need to take that precaution any time you have kids in a residence with guns," he said.

I fold up the *Examiner* and slide it under the sofa for safekeeping. Why do they gotta go and call me Dorothea, huh? Now everybody's gonna be like, "Dorothea, Dorothea," when they know good and well my name is Dimple, plain and simple. Sheez. What next?

Gives you the creeps to read about your own flesh and blood in the newspaper. It doesn't sound like they're talking about Dale at all, but just using his name to tell about somebody else. Seems like

Dale's gonna come bouncing down the steps any minute now, hollering, "Joke's on you, joke's on you," laughing like a fool.

Dale's got a big-time laugh, that's for sure. When we came out, he was the one blessed with the laugh, Mama always says, and I was the one blessed with the mouth.

I go into the kitchen and dig around for something to eat. Sunday is pancakes day, but I'm way too hungry to wait on 'em. A few saltines and a fun-size Milky Way oughta tie me over real good. Dale and me wonder why they call such dinky stuff fun-size? Seems like a candy bar oughta be at least a jumbo to qualify. I decide to wash down my breakfast with a glass of skim milk, to balance off the calories.

Then I'm back in the living room again, pulling the paper out of hiding, to study it over for the details. By now I know it cannot be true. At least not in the way they wrote it.

Take Nintendo, for starters. Ronnie Delaney doesn't have Nintendo. And even if he did, why would Dale and him want to play it? This makes no kinda sense at all. Ronnie's got a *Super* Nintendo. There's such a huge difference. Your graphics. Your controls. Whole different games. So right there the *Examiner*'s dead wrong.

Then this other thing. They say it was a .22-caliber bullet. Dale's the one who told me himself a .22's no more powerful than a big old popgun. It just scares folks, he says. Won't kill 'em. Maybe you might shoot a pigeon or something with a .22, but not people. So right there's mistake number two.

Worst of all, the paper goes, "They're not releasing the name of the other child." Well, if they know so much down at the *Examiner*, how come they're not releasing that other name? Does this make sense to you? Nuh-uh. No way.

I fold up the paper, neating along the edges, and toss it onto the hassock. Stupid mix-up is what it looks like to me. You might think the *Cuthbur Examiner* would care to get their details right, it being the only newspaper we got.

It *could* be my brother died, I know that. But then maybe he didn't. They got the story dead wrong, that's all I'm saying. And when you get your details wrong, who can tell what else might go up in smoke? The whole darn thing could go *ka-blooey*. Maybe.

When Daddy comes downstairs, I'm waiting for him with the good news.

"Ronnie's got *Super* Nintendo," I go.

"What, honey?" His eyes are all red from rubbing 'em.

"Ronnie's got him a Super Nintendo."

"Come on, Dimple. You know Mama and me can't afford to buy you no Super Nintendo. We already gone round 'bout that."

"No, no, I'm not asking for Super Nintendo. Me and Dale don't even want one anymore."

Daddy shuffles into the parlor, wearing his Sunday slippers, and squeezes a arm around my shoulder.

I'm like, "Look at the paper there," pointing at the hassock.

He unclasps me and picks it up for himself, studying the headline.

I can't wait for him to read through the story, so I spill the beans. "They got it all wrong, Daddy. Screwed up the details so bad, makes you want to laugh."

"What are you talking about, Dimple?"

"They say Dale and Ronnie were playing with Nintendo. That's not true. Ronnie doesn't even have Nintendo. He's got *Super* Nintendo."

Daddy nods at me, still not catching on.

"They say it was a twenty-two-caliber bullet," I go. "But you can't kill somebody with a twenty-two. Dale told me so himself. He can't be dead."

Daddy plops down on the sofa staring at me, astonished by my brainpower.

I finish him off by slapping the *Examiner* clean outta his hands. "They don't even name Ronnie Delaney. Me they gotta go and call Dorothea."

Daddy's like, "Dimple?" patting the sofa next to where he's sitting.

"What?" I go, smiling and pleased with myself, even though I know it's like bragging.

"Sit down here, sweetheart."

I sit down next to him.

Daddy picks up the paper from off the floor where I slapped it down. He smooths it out on his knees. Then he points across the top, underlining the words with his finger: CUTHBUR YOUTH DIES IN SHOOTING. "That's your brother, Dimple. There's no mistake."

"But . . ."

Daddy jabs his finger at the headline and says it again. "Dale is dead, sweetheart. Nothing I can do. Nothing you can do." His voice is sliding higher, sounding like that squeak when Ivy June tries to blow her clarinet. Then I see how he's starting to cry.

Not me, brother. No way. Dimple and Dale are no criers.

CHAPTER THREE

Dale and me got a secret club named Twin Protectors. Only we call it just TP, to throw people off the scent and make 'em think about toilet paper. We came up with the idea that first summer our family moved into Cuthbur from Alto Pass. We were the new kids in town, and everybody wanted to make fun of us. It was like they had never seen or heard of twins before. Like we were freaks or something. Belonged in a carnival. This was the stated opinion of our neighbor, Reginald Something-or-Other, who ended up paying full price for his opinion to the tune of a fat lip.

Reginald's daddy landed a new job at the end of that first summer, and they moved out of Cuthbur. No loss.

Our club's got two officers—President and Social Director. The first one calls the meetings. The second one collects the dues. Dale ran for President. I ran for Social Director. We both won by a landslide.

Truth to tell, Cuthbur's not such a tough town when you come right down to it. Only we couldn't tell that at the beginning. Being born in Alto Pass and growing up there through the third grade, Dale and me had some pretty funny ideas about Cuthbur. For starters, it seemed so *big*—near six thousand folks. Right there you're up against a attitude called know-it-all. Then it's got a football team and Alto Pass doesn't, so there's another thing. Then, to top it off, it's got all the fancy shops for miles around, so some folks become all la-di-da and snotty, crazy for fashion.

To say nothing about the name Cuthbur itself, which sounds like the whole town talks with a lisp. "Thee the movie: *Cuthbur'th Lath Thtand.*" Every time I say this, Dale cracks up.

But, really, Cuthbur isn't all that bad. After you get used to it, it's pretty nice.

Our motto for Twin Protectors comes out like a poem, copped off a hymn down at the Baptist church, wrote by our Social Director (that's me) and repeated at the start of every meeting by our President (that's him):

> *Blest be the tie that binds*
> *Our hearts up in Christian love*
> *Mess with a twin—don't matter which one—*
> *Look out for that pie that blinds.*

Anybody who knows this song can sing along because the words fit perfect. It's only the last line that drives me crazy.

When I was writing it, I got stuck for something that could blind somebody and fit in the middle. Anything at all. For our first few meetings we sung "knuckle sandwich." Then I got inspired with this idea for a pie. Just hit me out of the blue.

As soon as everybody in Cuthbur figured out we meant business, there wasn't so much need for Twin Protectors anymore. But, at the start, we had to prove it. If somebody ragged on me—like maybe they went "Dimple's simple"—then Dale would come through right away and smack 'em. Or if somebody ragged on him—maybe going, "Siamese Twins, half girl–half boy"—then I had to come right through and smack *them*.

Twin Protectors has only one rule: "Never delay a payback." If one of us needs protecting, then the other one's gotta deliver the goods pronto. Smack.

Matter of fact, this is how we met up with Ronnie Delaney. All three of us became best friends not long after the blood dried. It was the first day of school, out on the playground for recess, when Ronnie called Dale a "hick from Alto Pass," for no good reason at all. I heard what he said the first time, but I decided to give him a second chance. He seemed like such a little squirt to have to flatten right outta the blue like that. I went, "What'd you call my brother?"

And Ronnie repeated the word, like a stupid idiot. He probably wasn't expecting any trouble off some girl.

But as soon as I heard "hick" for a second time, I jumped him.

I'm taller than Ronnie is. But then he's tougher than he looks. He smacked me straight across the mouth and split my lip open. Blood started dripping on the inside and on the outside both.

Of course, just as soon as Dale noticed this, it was like he started seeing red. First he pulled me off Ronnie, and then he started slapping the kid across his cheeks—smack on the left, smack on the right. Hard.

Dale was screaming, "If you even *think* about hitting my sister again, Twin Protectors are gonna take out a contract on your kneecaps, son!"

Dale loves to call people "son" when he's real ticked at 'em. But more than anything else, he wishes we had a legal department for Twin Protectors. Somebody who could make good on all our contracts.

The principal suspended us all for three days

for fighting. Ronnie and Dale and me agreed this was unfair punishment just for getting acquainted. So, to show her, we began hanging out together. It wasn't then when I let Ronnie kiss me. But it was back that far when him and Dale and me became best friends.

With what's happened now, everything's got to change, of course. I wish I didn't have to do a job on Ronnie, I really do. But twins are twins, and a promise is a promise. When it comes right down to it, blood's thicker than all get-out.

Mama doesn't come downstairs Sunday morning till near ten o'clock. Daddy and me have already decided to skip church. She doesn't wanta look at the newspaper, she says. She doesn't feel like making pancakes, she says. She doesn't wanta eat anything herself, she says.

"You got to keep your strength up, Doris," Daddy goes.

And she says, "Strength for *what*?"—sounding like the queen of sarcasm.

He answers back in that quiet voice he's got. "Strength for the visitation. Strength for the funeral."

I never thought about either of these before. "What visitation?" I go.

Mama doesn't wanta talk about it, so she escapes into the bathroom. Starts running water into the tub.

I feel like apologizing to her for smartin' off last night, but I don't see an opening.

Daddy motions for me to sit down with him at the kitchen table. "Visitation's a time at the funeral parlor tonight," he says.

I keep my mouth shut, seeing how he's in a mood to talk.

"Use to call it a wake, but now it's just a visitation."

"Okay," I go.

"A time for folks to come by and pay their respects, you know."

"Respects to who?"

"To your mama. To you and me. And to Dale, of course."

"Dale's gonna be there?"

"Well, sure he is, honey. His body's gonna be there. Down at Bert's Funeral Parlor."

Just then the telephone rings, and Daddy goes to answer it, leaving me alone to mull over this idea of a visitation. Truth to tell, I'm not ignorant when it comes to the word. I know what it means. Just asked to make sure.

I've been to Bert's before, too, when Grandpa—

that's Mama's half-daddy—passed. The place was pure beautiful, 'cause it's actually Bert's Funeral Parlor and Furniture Emporium. They got these posh chairs and sofas—prettiest in Cuthbur—making the place look like some kinda palace.

I remember how Mama was all worried Dale and me were gonna puke or something when we laid eyes on Grandpa Clarence at his funeral, laid out in that coffin with the lid up. Sheez. There ain't nothing to it. A corpse just looks like some wax dummy at the carnival. I leaned over during the funeral and told Mama, "I find this interesting," which seemed like it made *her* wanta puke.

Daddy comes back from the phone.

"Who was that?" I go.

"The paper."

"*Cuthbur Examiner*?"

"That's right."

"Did you tell 'em about the Super Nintendo?"

"No, Dimple. They don't want to know about no Super Nintendo. They want a obituary for Dale."

"Sheez."

"Mama and me got to write one and call 'em back."

"Let me write it for you," I go. "I can write good."

30

Daddy nods his head like he's thinking about this.

"Where were we, now?" he goes.

"Telling me about the visitation tonight."

Daddy lets out with a big sigh, sounding more tuckered than after a week at the meat-packing plant. "It's gonna be at six o'clock, but you don't have to go if you don't feel like it, Dimple."

"I want to go."

"We could take you over to Sheila's or Ivy June's, if you don't want to go along."

Sheila is my best friend in the whole world. Ivy June, as you already know, is not.

"But I *want* to go."

"You don't have to."

Daddy's talking to me with his eyes closed, he's so tired.

I get up and give him a pat on the shoulder before heading for my own bedroom to write Dale's obituary.

It musta taken me an hour 'cause when I come back down, Mama's all done with her bath. Daddy and her are sitting together in the parlor.

Mama goes, "Dimple?"

"What?"

"Come in here with Daddy and me."

I walk into the parlor carrying my piece of

notebook paper and stand in front of 'em.

"Sit down there," Mama goes, nodding at the hassock.

I do.

She's trying to look me in the eye but having a hard time of it. "I'm real sorry I snapped at you last night, sweetie," she goes. "You know I love you and . . ."

She wants to say Dale's name, too, but can't do it. Instead, she clouds up and begins to bawl. Daddy puts an arm around her for comfort while I just sit there and wait.

I notice nobody puts an arm around me for comfort. It probably wouldn't strike 'em to try this. I'm not that easy to put an arm around.

When Mama settles down, I go, "Wanta hear my obituary?"

She snuffles some snot, trying to smile at me. I know how that goes, so I wait a minute for the flow to slow.

Mama's like, "Go ahead, baby."

Daddy nods, so I start in reading.

Honest, I figure they're gonna like it. I sure don't mean any harm by it. But seems like they always take my writing the wrong way. See what you think.

*Dale Dorfman, only son of Marvin and Doris,
beloved brother of Dimple, got shot dead at the
house of Ronnie Delaney on Saturday while
playing Super Nintendo. It was a big-caliber
gun. Nobody was there to stop it, including the
next-door neighbor, Miss Ivy June Fishback.*

*Dale was a Boy Scout with four badges. He
could play the cornet and came in second
place last year in the Cuthbur Elementary
spelling bee, confusing a "t" with a "s" in the
word "caution," and losing out to Florio
Capecci. He was President of a secret club, but
we will not release the name of it.*

*Dale will be missed by Marvin and Doris
and even more by his sister Dimple. They are
still twins.*

*This crime is under investigation. Do not mess
with firearms.*

CHAPTER FOUR

It's a relief to climb into our car and drive down to Bert's Funeral Parlor and Furniture Emporium, just so we can get outta the house. The phone rung like crazy all day long. Nearly exhausted Mama and frazzled Daddy's nerves to a razor edge.

On the ride downtown, Mama goes, "You don't gotta stay in the waking parlor with him if you don't want to, Dimple."

"With Dale, you mean?"

"Uh-huh. They got this lobby where you can go and sit if you want to, sweetheart."

She's being real nice. Very considerate.

Still, I can't stop myself from asking her, "What's the point of going to a visitation if I'm gonna sit in the lobby the whole time, huh?"

"I'm only telling you what you can do if you want to, honey, that's all. It's gonna be a long evening."

I don't say anything back to this, so they'll feel free to talk alone in the front seat. I'd like to say something sweet myself, something kind, but I

34

don't have much practice at it. Silence is the best I can come up with.

Up in front, Mama's saying how this car needs washing, and Daddy promises he'll do it tomorrow before the funeral.

Me, I figure washing an old Malibu Classic is something of a waste on any day.

When Mama says she wishes it was washed already, I can't help chiming in on Daddy's side. "He's been busy all day long," I go. "Running to the funeral parlor, talking to the insurance people, calling up the newspaper and stuff. When did you think he was going to wash this car, huh?" I hear my own nastiness and wonder where it comes from. Wish I could ditch it.

"Leave it alone now, Dimple," Daddy goes, taking Mama's side once I jump in on his.

I'm like, "It doesn't matter to Dale anyhow if you wash this car or not."

"Please, Dimple," Daddy goes, "just leave it be."

I wish I could leave it be. Instead I say a swear word real low, so they won't hear me.

"What was that?" Mama goes, almost too tired to care.

"Nothing," I fib. "I didn't say nothing."

"Well, you better not of. I know you're upset, sweetheart. We all are. But that's no reason to—"

"She didn't say it, Doris," Daddy goes, covering for me.

We keep rolling along for a while without any more talk. I'm thinking to myself how Dale and me like to ride together in the backseat on a long trip. We play this secret alphabet game with road signs. When he spots an "A" he mouths some dirty word starting with that letter, but don't make any sound so only I can hear him. When I spot a "B" on a sign, I lip another dirty word beginning with that letter, for his ears only. Mama and Daddy never catch on how we got this whole alphabet of wash-your-mouth-out vocabs from A to Z. Try it yourself. Some of those letters aren't so easy, believe me.

When Daddy turns left onto Main Street, I'm thinking silent to Dale, "I got 'M' for 'men-o'-paws.' "

Up in the front seat, Daddy's going, "We don't know what he's gonna look like, Dimple, so don't be surprised when you see him."

I hear my name.

"Who? Dale?"

"Yes, honey. Dale."

I'm like, "He's gonna look like a kid with a bullet in him, that's what."

Mama starts squealing bloody murder at this.

"Sorry," I shout back at her. "But it's the truth."

36

"Please don't say that, Dimple," she bawls at me. "Don't ever say that again, okay?"

Daddy goes, "Can we have some peace and quiet in this car, the both of yous?"

I pretzel my arms across my chest and lock down my jaw. I really didn't mean to hurt Mama's feelings by smart-mouthing her. Still, facts is facts, the way I look at it, and I wish Daddy or Mama would let loose with a few of those precious facts they're keeping secret from me.

We get there about five thirty, a full thirty minutes before opening time for visitation. This is so we can look at Dale by ourselves and get used to the sight of his body before company comes. The minute you walk through that front door, you just know you're in a funeral parlor. That or Bob's Florist, take your pick. It stinks to high heaven to where you can hardly inhale. No wonder corpses hold their breath.

"Whew," I go.

And Mama's like, "Smells heavenly, don't it?"

Sheez.

Mr. Bert, the funeral director, comes outta his office to meet us. He's wearing a high-class black suit that puts Daddy's old brown one to shame.

I forgot to tell you how Mama's got herself all dolled up in last year's Easter dress with these pink polka dots set on a field of black. She believes such a dress is fitting for funerals *and* resurrections, if you gaze on the polka dots with the eyes of faith. Looks like it might be better matched to a fancy roller rink if you ask me, but I keep this opinion to myself.

I'm wearing my green plaid skirt, green sweater, and green knee socks. Dale knows my favorite color.

"I believe you will be pleased," Mr. Bert tells Mama and Daddy, once we're all standing in his lobby. "Your boy's at rest."

I cough so Mr. Bert will look my way.

"Dale's dead," I remind him.

"Eternal rest, pretty girl," he says back, smiling down.

This frosts me, but Daddy's smart enough to put a hand on my shoulder before I lip off. If I go and pop this funeral director one, it's probably gonna add more to the bill. Instead, I just squint my eyes up into his pinched face. In secret, though, I'm adding up how much money Dale and me got in the dues box of Twin Protectors. Maybe I could pop him one and pay for the damages myself.

Mama begins to cry as soon as we walk into the parlor. "Boo-hoo," she goes. "Don't he look like a picture?"

She musta learned this line outta some old movie, 'cause it sounds fake to me.

I lay back and let them take the first peek. Dale's coffin is clear at the other end of the room, but I don't choose to look at it yet. There are flowers all over the place, lined up in white buckets clamped into brass holders. Big chairs set like thrones along the walls. Seems you could squeeze most of Cuthbur into this one room if you wanted to.

"Come on, rose petal," Mr. Bert goes.

I look around to see who he's talking to. Ain't nobody else in the room 'cept me. Sheez. "Rose petal"? I got a mind to take Daddy's pruning shears and snip that man's buds clean off his vine.

Mama's staring back at me now. "Don't be afraid to look, sweetheart."

Did you hear that, Dale, lying up there right next to her? Who does she think she's talking to, anyway? Dimple Dorfman afraid? Oh, right. Hah.

I march up to the coffin and elbow my way in between Mama and Daddy. She reaches out to take one of my hands, but I clasp 'em both in front of me so she can't do it.

I know I oughta be looking down into Dale's face, but I can't do that. Not now. Not yet. There's no way they're gonna see me cry. Dale understands how Twin Protectors can't go soft before a payback. First things first.

Mama goes, "He looks good, don't he?"

"I think so," Daddy agrees.

"Not an easy case," Mr. Bert says. "We hope you're pleased."

I'm like, "Where's the bullet hole?"

"Shhh," Mama goes.

Daddy grips my shoulder. "We can talk about that later, just you and me."

"Mr. Bert," I ask him, "what did you do with the bullet?"

"Dimple."

"Sorry, Mama, but I want to know where it is."

Mr. Bert can't tell whether to answer me or not.

"Do you still got it? Because I want it if you got it."

"Dimple."

"It belongs to us," I remind everybody.

I figure if no one's gonna tell me the whole story, the least they can do is hand over the bullet. I need that bullet.

"We don't have the bullet," Mr. Bert explains. "I believe the police would have kept it after the autopsy."

I turn to Daddy. "It's ours by rights, you know."

He nods. I notice how his eyes are closed.

"Where's the hole, then?" I wanta know.

Mama pulls out a polka dot hankie from her dress sleeve and starts dabbing at her eyes.

"Would you like me to answer the girl?" Mr. Bert asks Daddy.

He looks from me to Mama and then back to me again, not sure what to recommend. Finally he goes, "Yes, please," like he's asking for some kind of favor.

Mr. Bert uses his official voice now, pretending he's a doctor or something. "The hole would not be visible," he goes, looking at me like I'm dim-witted.

"I can see it isn't visible. Do you think I'm blind?"

"Please, Dimple," Mama goes. "Mind your manners."

"Sorry."

Mr. Bert tells me, "The bullet entered his body on the right side of the chest, three inches below the collarbone."

"You mean Dale's *pit*?"

Mr. Bert nods, but I can tell he doesn't care for my vocabulary.

"Then it traveled through the lung and pierced the heart."

"Is that where it ended up? In his heart?"

"I believe so."

I stand there staring down at Dale, trying to see clean through his blue suit with the too-short sleeves, and the white shirt he hates so, to where the bullet hole is. I let my eyes go blurry, so I won't see his face. I'm not ready for that yet.

"Thank you," I say. "I wished to know it."

"You're welcome," Mr. Bert goes, glad that it's over.

I want to ask him if he ever gets a corpse in with a bullet hole to the face. How do they handle that, I wonder? Do you think they'd ever bury somebody in a ski mask? Or maybe plug up the hole and paint over it to look like some kinda big mole?

Folks start filing in right at the stroke of six. Cuthbur is a on-time town.

Aunt Nell and Uncle Lucky come from over in Alto Pass.

Francine—that's Daddy's lulu sister—gets the night off from the bowling alley and swishes in with her bartender friend, who Mama can't stand.

Mr. Quick—Dale's and my sixth-grade teacher—comes too, which just about knocks me over from surprise. He can't think of one single thing to say. There's a first.

When Sheila comes in, she makes her way straight over to me. Even though she's in the seventh grade and twice as grown up as I'll ever be, it's hard on her to be in a funeral parlor, I can tell. Her eyes are all watery and red. She's so sweet, Sheila is.

Back when we moved into Cuthbur, she was the first person who stood up for me, outside of Dale. It happened in P.E. when her class of girls was playing dodgeball against us. I was the last girl standing on our side. They had four or five still left. Sheila wasn't one of them, of course, on account of her lacking the meanness to be a really good dodgeball player. (I happen to be blessed on that score myself.)

Being outnumbered so bad, I broke into my warrior scream, picked up two balls, and started charging at 'em head-on. I whipped one ball, then the other. As soon as I ran out of ammo, I scrambled for more. I was throwing balls as hard as I could, aiming high.

Finally, it came down to just one of them left standing against me. All their girls were cheering for Marybelle Kunkle. All my girls were screaming for me. Now, I'll give you two guesses who took a ball right in the gut, then flopped down on the gym floor with the wind knocked clean out of her?

After that game, Marybelle Kunkle started the rumor that she'd lost on purpose, because her chest is so well endowed and it needs protection. She also told everybody I was as flat-chested as a boy, and even flatter-chested than some boys she could name.

So what if this was true? I say it has nothing to do with who whipped who in dodgeball. Fact is, I beat Marybelle fair and square.

The next day in gym class all the girls wanted Marybelle and me to strip and compare. That's when Sheila came to my rescue. Real loud, she went, "Dimple's chest is *ample*. I've seen it. And anyway, comparisons are *odious*." Just like that.

That was the day I learned how big words well aimed can punch as powerful as any fist. *Ample. Odious.* Sheez.

When Pastor Fuller comes into the funeral parlor he takes command, moving all around the room and shaking hands. Seems like he's warming up for the service tomorrow, practicing that line over and over about "though I walk through the valley of death and cast no shadow."

Sheriff McNally is present, too, sliding along the walls, moving like a garter snake. He isn't in uniform, so I try to spot through his suit if he's packing a rod or not. Looks like a bulge in there to me. I keep my eyes open for the right time to go over and ask him about my bullet.

Everybody's being extra nice. Hugging on me. Kissing on me. Crying and saying how they're gonna do anything in the world for me. Talking about heaven. They all mean well.

Then, along about eight o'clock, with there being just one hour more to go, who do you think comes standing in the doorway to our funeral parlor, big as life? I gotta rub my eyes to make sure myself.

There she is, posing like some kinda beauty queen from hell—Miss Ivy June Fishback.

I'm standing next to the coffin when I spot her. She's clear across the room. There's a zillion folks between us, but I zero in on her like one of those scud missiles. All the way toward her, as I'm weaving through the crowd, I keep repeating to myself Rule Number One of Twin Protectors: "Never delay a payback."

Never ever.

CHAPTER FIVE

Ivy June is wearing this pink velvet hat. Looks like a pie plate with earflaps. She sees me coming at her and grabs hold of the top of it for extra protection. When I reach her, I wrap my arms around and give her a big bear hug, pressing up against her chest-to-chest. From there, I can grab two big handfuls of hair outta the back of her head, and I start yanking.

She screeches to kingdom come, but nobody dares step near the two of us. They all believe we're bosom buddies wailing in grief because my brother has died.

I whisper straight into Ivy June's ear. "Next time I ask you a question, girl, you better give me a answer real quick."

"I will, I will," she squeals.

I keep ahold of her hair and whisper some more. "Whatever happened to Dale last night, the truth of it belongs to me. You got that? It's not *your* story. It's not anybody else's story. It's *mine*. And that means *all* of it. Every detail."

"Okay, okay," Ivy June goes, trying to twist out from under my tight grip. Good luck, girl.

It takes Mama to suspicion the truth of what's happening, how I'm actually scalping Ivy June. She comes over and pulls us apart.

I don't leave any holes in Ivy June's head, and there ain't no blood. Heck, I don't want to hurt her. Just want to get her attention. Of course, I do manage to mess up her perm pretty good.

She starts in screaming how she's injured—blah-blah-blah—and then all of a sudden notices how the long hairs I'm twisting between my fingers happen to be the same color as hers.

"*Aaahhhh*," she hollers. "*Aaahhh*."

Mrs. Fishback—that's Ivy June's mama—moves alongside and puts a comforting hand on her daughter's shoulder, thinking she's overcome by grief. "There, there."

"Dimple pulled out all my hair," Ivy June wails.

I shake my head real slow from side to side, looking sad. "Some folks get hysteric," I tell her mama. "I wouldn't hold it against her, if I was you."

Mrs. Fishback goes, "Pull yourself together, young lady, and say something nice to Dimple."

"Why should I?" Ivy June cries. "She pulled out all my hair. On purpose."

Her mama's shocked at this bald-faced lie. "In a funeral parlor?" she scolds Ivy June. Mrs. Fishback

47

knows I might scalp somebody on their own front porch or up in a tree, but she doesn't figure even Dimple Dorfman is so savage as to go on the warpath in a funeral parlor.

"Don't pay her any mind," I go, dripping with the milk of human kindness.

Mrs. Fishback straightens up an inch taller, and I can tell it's hard for her to stand at the receiving end of somebody else's heartfelt sympathy. "We are *so* sorry for your loss, Dimple."

"Thank you," my mama butts in.

Mrs. Fishback pokes Ivy June in the gut so she'll say something sweet, but this doesn't appear likely. I stare straight at her, smothering her with my sad eyes.

Her mama goes, "Don't you have something nice to say to Dorothea?"

I let the name business pass, seeing how I really did pull Ivy June's hair.

Ivy June reaches a hand up to rub the back of her head, making like it still pains her. Then we all gotta wait while she thinks up what to say next. She squints her eyes at me and goes, "I told you Dale was hurt bad, didn't I?"

"Ivy June!" Mrs. Fishback gasps. She looks like she wants to smack somebody for her lack of manners.

Now my mama's insulted and goes, "Well, I never."

This seems like the moment for me to hold out the right hand of fellowship. "It's okay," I go, smoothing my words thick as Karo syrup.

Mama surprises me now by sticking up for Dale. "It is *not* all right," she goes. "Not in the presence of the deceased, it is *not* all right."

This doesn't sound one bit like my mama, who was born with a timid tongue. Not like Dale and me, who got us a pair of smart mouths.

I touch Mama on the elbow and shuffle us both away, feeling prouder of her right then than I have in a long time. She's shaking all over from hurt feelings and pure disgust. She leans down into my ear and whispers, "You were the picture of patience back there, baby. Who could blame you if you *did* pull out all of Ivy June's hair?"

I hand Mama off to Daddy and turn back around. From the distance I'm standing, it looks like Mrs. Fishback and Ivy June are locked in some kind of contest. They're in each other's faces with neither one of 'em budging an inch. I suppose I should feel sorry for what I did, but sorry is one thing in short supply right now. All I got of it I'm using on myself.

For the rest of the hour, till it's time for Bert's

Funeral Parlor to close up, I sit down on a folding chair next to Sheila. We could of taken a couple of plush chairs, on account of my being Dale's twin sister and almost the guest of honor, you could say. But Sheila's already sitting on a folding chair, and I figure a pinch of humbleness might do me some good.

Sheila reaches over and presses her cool fingers against my hot hands. "You holding up, Dimple?" she asks.

"Sure, I'm holding up," I tell her.

"No, really," she says. "You can tell me."

"Holding up just fine. Maybe a little tired," I admit. "That's all."

"Sure you are," Sheila says, letting her voice go kinda musical. "Uh-huh." She doesn't waste any words but starts rubbing her coolness into the heat of my hands. I never felt anything better in my whole life.

I glance up toward the coffin and let my eyes settle onto Dale's face. It's the first time I've looked at him without somebody else looking at me. His face is still. Real still. You know how some folks say dying is like going to sleep? Well, don't believe 'em. Dale doesn't appear to be sleeping to me. Not one bit. When he's asleep, Dale's face is full of life. Twitching, wrinkling up, pumping blood under his skin and through his cheeks. I've seen my brother asleep a hundred times, and he didn't look like this at all.

I stare up at him and notice how my own lips begin to press together real tight, trying to match his face. Even sitting here in Bert's Funeral Parlor and Furniture Emporium, Dale and me got the same mask. Twins forever.

Sheila keeps stroking my hands.

"You're sure sweet, Sheila."

"Mmmm," she hums.

I tilt my head back and let my eyes slide shut, feeling dead tired all of a sudden.

I whisper a nasty name, knowing Sheila will understand who I mean by it.

She keeps rubbing my hands, trading in her coolness for my heat, like pouring soothing water over them.

"Ivy June is that, all right," she agrees, filling in the blank.

Even though Sheila's got a vocabulary twice as big as mine, it does not happen to include this one word.

"Dimple?"

"What?"

"You can't be blaming Ivy June for what happened to Dale, you know. It won't do you any good. She didn't kill him."

I raise up my head at this remark and look around for a good place to spit. I feel the need.

Sheila says it again. "She didn't kill him, Dimple."

"Sheez."

I don't see any suitable spot. Spit's probably gonna stain their carpet anyways, and then Daddy'll have to pay for that, too. I elect to swallow it instead.

Sheila untwists her cool fingers from outta my clammy hands. It just about knocks me outta my chair when she goes, "You got one thing right. Ivy June is a . . ."

"Wash your mouth out, girl."

Ronnie Delaney's who killed my brother. The more I think about it, the surer I am. He doesn't come to the visitation, so I gotta wait at least another day to deliver what's coming to him. Truth to tell, I'm kinda relieved to have to delay this assignment. Doing Ronnie is gonna be my final contract for Twin Protectors, my last payback. After it's done, so is the club. After I do Ronnie, there won't be nothing more to do. Then Dale can rest in peace, and I'll be all alone.

I reach one of my own hands over on top of

Sheila's and squeeze. I look up at Dale's coffin again, then close my eyes. I tell myself to think of something else. Don't think about him being dead.

When Dale and me aren't out revenging on some enemy, or else sneaking walnuts outta Mr. Guzman's yard to sell down at the farmer's market on Saturdays, we like to play cutthroat games of Clue. You know the game? It's got Mrs. White and Professor Plum and Miss Peacock, all pretending they're murder suspects who bumped somebody off with this candlestick or rope or knife, while they were in the ballroom or library or kitchen. You gotta guess who done it, with what kinda weapon, and in what room. The answer's hid on these three cards tucked inside a secret black envelope.

Dale's got powerful hunches when it comes to playing Clue. Me, I zero in on the details, crossing out all the wrong answers before nailing the right dude. Three times outta four Dale beats me because he skips ahead and guesses before knowing the answer for sure. But then that one time I'll beat him because he might of missed a clue, and I don't hurry so fast. We marvel at each other's ways. I want to get quicker like Dale. He aims to get surer like me. There again we're twins, see? Match up perfect, only opposite.

I open my eyes. Sitting in the funeral parlor,

staring up at my brother's face and feeling the soft touch of Sheila's hand on mine, I'm ready to guess which three cards are inside the black envelope. I already know where it happened—in the bedroom. I already know what the weapon was—some sort of supercharged .22-caliber gun. And I'm zeroing in on who pulled the trigger.

I'd give a million bucks to be wrong. Heck, I'd give *two* million bucks not to have to kill Ronnie.

Sheila lets go of my hands and reaches up to stroke my head. She does it just once, only for a moment, but it sure feels fine.

CHAPTER SIX

None of us talks on the ride home, we're all so pooped. You wouldn't think something called a visitation could be such hard work. Not when all you have to do is sit around and talk to folks. But it is. It's very hard work. Probably because of who you gotta talk to—like Ivy June—and who isn't talking at all. Like Dale.

Back at the house, I can tell Mama and Daddy are running on empty. He keeps blowing breath out through his mouth in a steady stream of sighs. Maybe this is Morse code for Daddy's pain: dot d-a-s-h, dot d-a-s-h, inhale e-x-h-a-l-e. Mama's shoulders are drooped so low you'd think her dress might slip right off 'em. Even being this tired, she still says to Daddy and me, "How 'bout a glass of milk, you two? Maybe we got some Oreos left."

I answer, "No, thanks," thinking they'd rather go to bed and are just being nice.

But Daddy puts his hand on my shoulder and gives a little squeeze. "Come on, Dimple. When have you ever turned down a Oreo?"

We go into the kitchen together. Mama pours

the milk. Daddy gets the cookies out of the cupboard. There's half a line of Oreos left. Once, Dale and me finished off a whole package at a executive meeting of Twin Protectors. As Social Director, I'm in charge of refreshments and usually choose Oreos, even though the President's favorite happens to be vanilla wafers. At one meeting, he introduced a motion requiring us to eat Oreos and vanilla wafers every other time. It failed by a single vote.

"There sure were a lot of people there, Doris," Daddy says.

We're all sitting at the kitchen table. I notice how each of us looks at Dale's empty chair and then looks away.

"So many friends," Mama agrees.

"I couldn't believe Mr. Quick came," I go.

"He's a good teacher," Mama says.

"Good man," Daddy adds.

Then we all fall silent. There's nothing more to say. Nothing that's safe to say. Nobody chooses to mention the sight of Dale in his coffin. Nobody chooses to mention my scene with Ivy June. Nobody chooses to mention Ronnie Delaney not being there, or the sheriff sneaking in, or a hundred other things that would be too hard to talk about.

"I'm glad Sheila was with you," Mama goes.

"Yeah," I say. "Me too."

Daddy starts sighing again, puffing air out through his mouth. I don't think he knows he's doing it. Finally, he goes, "Have another Oreo, Dimple?"

I take one just to please him. Then I gulp down some milk. The darn cookie sticks in my throat. Doesn't wanta go all the way down.

Mama's eyes begin clouding over.

"Why don't you go to bed?" I tell her.

"You must be tired, too, honey," she goes. "Maybe that's what we all ought to do. Just go to bed."

"Pretty soon. I might watch some TV first."

Daddy says, "I'll stay down here with Dimple for a while."

"You don't have to," I tell him.

"I want to."

Mama pushes back her chair and stands up. She walks over to me and hugs my shoulders from behind. "I love you, sweetheart," she whispers into my ear.

I don't answer her in words but turn and kiss her cheek. Then she touches hands with Daddy and shuffles into the bathroom. Him and I get up and go into the living room.

What I really had in mind was getting some

time to myself, alone. I look into Daddy's eyes and see how tired they are. "Why don't you go to bed?" I say.

"Naw. None of us oughta be alone now. Not tonight."

I nod and switch on the TV, not noticing the programs as I dial around.

"That goes for Mama, too," I point out. "She's all alone upstairs."

"That's true."

Neither of us says who else is all alone. I wonder whether Daddy's thinking about Dale like I am. Lying in his coffin over there at the funeral parlor. Do they turn the lights out at Bert's, and would it be all dark inside? Or do they leave a light on somewhere? I can't think about it.

"There's nothing good on," I tell Daddy, switching off the TV.

"If you say so."

He doesn't move to get off the sofa until I head toward the stairs. He's waiting for me to go to bed first.

"Good night, Daddy."

I don't hear any answer from him, so I turn around and look. He's leaning his head into both his hands. He's blowing air out through his mouth again in that low sigh. I go over to him, wanting to say something, but I don't know the right words. So I just touch him on top of his head. On that little bald spot. He doesn't look up at me, but he knows what I mean.

This is the longest night I can remember in my whole life. I cannot fall asleep to save my soul. Mama comes into my room and checks on me. Then Daddy comes in and checks on me. I play possum both times, so they won't worry about me. Later, when I do fall asleep, it gets worse. I have horrible nightmares. I dream I'm lying inside Dale's coffin. I can't sit up. I keep staring at the silk lining puffing out of the lid. I wonder what it's gonna feel like when Mr. Bert closes it down. Even in my dream, I tell myself to stop thinking like this. But the dream goes on.

I don't cry out. That's one good thing. At least Mama and Daddy don't have to come running and see what's the matter.

I wake up long enough to squint at the sunrise and then fall back asleep.

The next thing I know, somebody's in my room talking. "Come on, honey. You can't sleep in today. Not this morning. I'm sorry."

It takes me a minute to come awake and see things straight.

"We gotta leave in one hour," Mama goes. "You better take your bath now and get some breakfast."

I open my eyes and see her standing next to my bed. Then I sit up. Oh, brother, did I ever sleep bad.

"Are you okay, honey?" Mama asks, leaning down and looking into my eyes.

"I'm okay," I tell her. My heart's racing.

"Gotta hurry, Dimple," Mama goes. "I'm sorry we couldn't let you sleep anymore. You were really sawing logs in here."

"What's the rush?" I ask her without thinking.

"We gotta leave for the funeral. I'm going downstairs now to run your bathwater. Please don't lay down again, sweetheart."

"I won't."

I stretch and yawn before swinging my legs out of the bed.

Mama walks down the steps. But then I hear her stop and call back up to me. "You're gonna need to wash your hair, Dimple. You can't just wet it."

I groan. Hair-washing oughta be a now-and-then thing, so's your hair won't wear out. I drag outta bed.

Sheila informed me that anybody who wants to go to Dale's funeral can skip school today with no penalty. This doesn't seem fair to me. A person shouldn't get a free day off school to go to Dale's funeral if they aren't his friend. Family oughta give out passes to a funeral, is what I believe. Funerals oughta be by invitation only.

I sort through my closet looking for what to wear and settle on my denim skirt with the black sweater. Dale and me dress to match sometimes, with him in his blue jeans and black sweatshirt. We've been saving up to buy identical black leather jackets when we turn thirteen. Gonna stitch "TP" on their backs and look awesome.

I take my bath before eating breakfast. Mama comes in to wash my hair, which I tell her isn't necessary, but she believes otherwise. Uses so much shampoo it's pure wasteful.

"How are all the children in China gonna wash their hair with us using up so many suds like this?" I go. But one thing about Mama is she doesn't care a lick about the children in China.

When I get back into my bedroom, somebody's laid out all different clothes. Here's my yellow dress spread over the bed with the tie belt and the stupid bow. I search around for where they hid my denim skirt.

I hate the yellow dress because it was purchased for me to play "Boogie-Woogie Cowboy" in. What a disaster that was. As soon as I sat down at the recital piano, with everybody's mom and dad staring up at me, my right hand forgot what it was supposed to be doing while the left hand kept on playing real good. Later, Ivy June banged out her "Spinning Wheel Song" perfect, and afterwards she's like, "If you'd practiced with both hands together, Dimple, that would never have happened to you." So I spilt my cherry Kool-Aid all over her dress by accident.

Now I wish I woulda spilt it on my own instead. A yellow dress with a big bow on its back just isn't me. No way. Looks all la-di-da and on display. 'Bout makes you wanta puke.

The church parking lot's almost full by the time our car pulls in there. Mr. Bert, the funeral director, is busy sliding purple flags onto the radio antennas of all the cars, or else plunking a magnet holder on the ones without radios. Mama explains to me how this marks which vehicles are gonna be in the funeral parade out to the cemetery. Daddy says so long as you got a purple flag, you can run a red light. It's the law.

The Baptist church is crammed full of people, just like on pack-the-pew night. Everybody and his brother is there. It stinks to kingdom come, with flowers fuming up the place almost as bad as in

Bert's Funeral Parlor and Furniture Emporium.

Mr. Shoofelt ushers Mama, Daddy, and me down the middle aisle, walking us real slow and solemn. It puts me in mind of a wedding, and I start wondering what it would feel like to get married.

I spot Sheila over to the left, looking real pretty and genuine sad. There's Ivy June on the right, showing off a brand-new hat and sitting next to her mama, who's wearing another fancy headdress. Makes her look like an Egyptian mummy. I believe Mrs. Fishback must have a discount card down at Helen's Hats and Hose, seeing how many bargains the two of them are always stacking on top of their heads.

Mama gets tipsy when we arrive near the front of the church and just about collapses into our pew. Daddy has to hold on to her and prop her up. She slides in first, then him, and I get to sit next to the aisle.

Dale's coffin is laid on a scooter deal with the wheels resting right where the communion table usually goes. The lid is up, and he's looking pretty puny. Maybe the lights are brighter in this Baptist church than they were over at Bert's Funeral and Furniture. These don't favor his coloring.

Old Miss Weatherby's pumping out organ

music to grieve by. Pastor Fuller always says it's a regular miracle how good she can play with so much arthritis in every joint. Of course, she's slow. Her first tune is "I Come to the Garden Alone."

I look over at Dale. He prefers "Onward Christian Soldiers," 'cause of how it makes him wanta stand up and march. Me, I go in for "He's Got the Whole World in His Hands," something with a little swing and sway to it.

It dawns on me all of a sudden how Dale probably just wants this thing to get over with.

I swivel around and look back at the people. Usually this would be rude, but when you're immediate family of a deceased person, you got rights. That's the moment I see *him*, sitting along the aisle about halfway back. I don't know how I coulda walked right past him on the way in and not of noticed. If Dale would care to turn his head a little to the right on that shiny pillow of his, he could spot him too.

Ronnie Delaney's staring straight up at my brother, with eyes all puffy and red from crying. Sheez. Can you believe it? What's *he* got to cry about?

I ask you, am *I* crying?

This isn't the way I'd hoped to meet Ronnie Delaney in a church someday, but sometimes even your best plans gotta change. It is my duty to Twin Protectors, pledged and sealed, to even the score with Ronnie Delaney. And I mean *today*. Our Social Director is not about to let her President down.

CHAPTER SEVEN

The funeral begins. I can't listen very close to the words Pastor Fuller is speaking about how the Lord is my shepherd, and no sparrow is gonna fall to the ground without God taking notice. Instead I'm staring up at Dale, thinking how I'm never gonna see my brother again once they close down that lid. Even with a bullet hole, I know I'm gonna miss the sight of him something awful.

A twin is a nutty thing to be, when you sit down and really think about it. You've got this double walking around, looking almost the same as you and talking just about alike. I'm not saying Dale and me are clones or anything like that, because we think extremely different on certain subjects. But then I'm not saying we're completely separate from each other either. Someplace deep down inside both of us we're connected, where nobody else can see it.

It's like this: When him and me are fighting each other, throwing fists and spitting spit, even then we're still connected because of being twins. Or maybe if I'm mad at him, all of a sudden it feels more like I'm mad at myself. Or if Dale stands up for me against some bully, it's more like he's standing up for hisself. It's the twins thing. We've talked about this, and Dale agrees with me. When you come right down to it, Twin Protectors is a whole lot more than some secret club. It's about our life together.

Now I'm staring up at him and wondering what it would feel like to lie in that coffin the way he is. Of course, I'm not stupid. I know Dale probably can't feel a thing. Still, if it was me up there in that box . . .

Maybe it would feel like sleeping on Mama's satin pillow, the pink one she uses to keep her poof-do from going lopsided between visits to Miss Earlene. That pillow of hers feels slip-slidey and cool, real good when you're in the mood.

But I don't choose to think about this anymore. I close my eyes, trying to block out the picture from my nightmare of Mr. Bert closing down the lid. Where does all the air go? It almost makes me puke worrying about this.

I open my eyes and force myself to think about something else. How would Dale feel if *he* was the one left out here, and it was me lying up there in the coffin? What if he was the one sitting in the Baptist church watching his own twin sister get funeraled? He'd be *devastated*, that's what. Flat-out devastated.

I'm not saying he'd bawl or anything. He'd probably feel like somebody had come up to him, hauled off and punched him right in the gut— *wump*—knocking all the wind out. And then he'd probably feel like somebody else, some complete stranger, had sneaked up from behind and walloped him in the head—*wap*. Then, after he fell down to the ground, he'd feel like both of 'em had jumped him and started beating on him. That's when it would hit him like a ton of bricks: Dimple's not coming to my rescue. These guys, whoever the heck they are, are gonna keep pounding on me and pounding on me till kingdom come because Dimple ain't here to stop 'em. Not this time. Not ever again.

And why's that?

Because Dimple's dead and gone, that's why.

I believe this is what Dale would be thinking if it was me lying up there, stretched out stiff as a wax dummy between those puffs of satin, and he was the one sitting out here listening to Mama sniffling her grief-snot, feeling Daddy's hot sighs pressing down next to him, and trying to get a grip on Pastor Fuller's thought about how "there's no such thing as a *accident* in God's eternal plan."

Oh yeah, and one more thing. If we switched places, my brother and me, Dale's blood would be boiling mad at whoever done it to me, you better believe that. This thought wakes me up all of a sudden. Kinda splashes me with a good douse of cold water. Fact is, Dale is *not* the one sitting in this Baptist church watching his twin sister get funeraled. Fact is, he is *not* the one with a chance to settle the score against Ronnie Delaney.

Fact is, *I'm* the one.

After Pastor Fuller finishes talking, he motions for all of us to stand up. Then he turns to Miss Weatherby and gives her the sacred sign to start pumping the organ for "When the Roll Is Called Up Yonder."

Everybody hoists themselves up and starts singing. Mama leans against Daddy's arm for a steadier. He pats her hand. I'm probably the only one in this whole church—and there's a mess of us here—who can't muster a single Christian thought. What I'm thinking is, Who needs to wait for "up yonder" to call the darn roll? I'm gonna call it right here and now.

So I take a giant step out into the middle aisle and look back over the congregation, zeroing my sights in on Ronnie Delaney. I can't say how many people notice me, because everybody is harmonizing to high heaven. But Ronnie sees me, you better believe. That much is for sure. He looks right into my eyes, and I stare back right into his. Maybe he's scared of me and maybe he's not. I can't tell.

I raise up my right arm real slow. I cock my thumb and stiffen my pointer finger till it's aimed straight at him, smack between his eyes.

"Dimple," Daddy calls out, yanking me back into our pew.

I see Ronnie flinch, even though I don't pull the trigger. Not this time, I don't.

Walking out of the church, Daddy puts one hand under Mama's arm and another one under mine. He wants to make sure she doesn't fall and I don't pull any funny business.

Outside, the three of us get to ride in a shiny black Lincoln Town Car. It's got gold letters painted on the door spelling BERT'S FUNERAL PARLOR AND FURNITURE EMPORIUM. This automobile stands second in line, right behind the hearse. It isn't a real limousine like they got in Hollywood, but it's darn close. Biggest car in Cuthbur, and I always wanted to see inside it.

The backseat's made outta gray leather, softer than a oiled ball glove and sporting about as much leg room as some folks' front parlors.

I climb in, hardly needing to duck my head, it's so big. "Can Sheila ride with us?"

Mama sits right next to me, but she doesn't answer. Maybe she didn't hear.

"Can Sheila come along?"

Daddy eases next to Mama and leaves the door open. Everybody coming outta the church can peer into our Lincoln Town Car, glimpsing the glory of it for theirselves. He goes, "This car is reserved for immediate family, Dimple."

"Do we have to pay extra," I ask him, "if a best friend rides along?"

"I wouldn't think so, honey."

I look over at Mama. She isn't exactly crying, but then she's not exactly rock solid, either. If she says no, I decide I won't press it.

Mama smiles at me and nods okay without speaking the word.

"All right then," Daddy goes. "You get Sheila if that's gonna make you feel better, Dimple."

I crawl back out over Mama's and Daddy's legs, forgetting there's a door on my side. I don't muss up their clothes any, seeing how luxurious everything is. Plenty of leg room.

At first Sheila doesn't think she oughta join us. But then Daddy motions for her to get in, and that seems to put her mind at ease. Sheila and me squeeze next to each other beside my window, and there's still plenty of room for Mama and Daddy. They're rubbing up together, trying to smooth some comfort into each other skin-to-skin. I can't say if it's working. Hope so.

"Isn't this something?" I whisper to Sheila. "Have you ever been in a Lincoln Town Car before?"

She shakes her head no, which is what I figured.

"A person could live their whole life in here," I go. "If they'd just install a john."

Sheila repeats, "In*stall*," pointing out the joke inside my word. "Maybe there's a two-staller locked in the trunk."

"You think so?"

"It's big enough for two."

I squash a giggle so I won't disrespect Dale. Sheila is so smart. And sweet. Not one bit snotty.

Looking out through Daddy's door, she whispers, "Trouble coming."

Sure enough, Ivy June and Mrs. Fishback are marching out of the church like mourners on parade. They're heading straight for our car. Mrs. Fishback pushes her head into the clean air of our backseat and touches Daddy's knee with her

72

fingertips. "How you holding up, Mr. Dorfman? Mrs. Dorfman?"

Daddy gives her a weak smile, but Mama doesn't bother. Neither of 'em answers.

"May the Lord give you shelter in this storm," Mrs. Fishback says, patting Daddy's knee some more before backing outta our space.

I'm thinking, "Who died and made her weatherman?" But I don't say this out loud.

Ivy June has a pained look splattered across her face. She's staring into our Lincoln Town Car with eyes full of envy. That or stomach gas.

Then I glance up at Sheila, and she's sticking her tongue out at Ivy June. Not more than an inch, mind you. Very ladylike.

After a minute, Mr. Bert and one of his helpers show up in the church door.

"Here comes Dale," I say.

This announcement jerks Mama's head to attention. Maybe she thinks she's gonna lay eyes on Dale himself instead of just his coffin. I should of chose a different word.

Dale's lid is closed down tight now. Mr. Bert must of done that part after everybody left the church. It's one thing I'm glad to miss.

They wheel Dale to the back of the hearse, give the coffin a nudge off the cart, then roll it smooth as

73

anything into place. Mr. Bert closes the door real slow and double-checks to make sure the handle isn't gonna jiggle open if they hit a pothole or something.

"Listen to her purr," I whisper to Sheila once our Lincoln Town Car revs up. Any minute now I expect to lower my electric window and have some rich Hollywood star tell me to hand over the fancy mustard.

Our ride to Cuthbur Municipal Cemetery goes fast, even though we don't push this baby over twenty miles per, outta respect for the dead. Mama and Daddy sit quiet the whole time, not speaking a word. Just leaning into each other. Along the way, she takes hold of his hand and I can tell they're both squeezing. Now and again, one of 'em looks my way and tries to smile.

I'm pressing my lips into Sheila's ear, cupping my hand for protection, and whispering different plans for nailing Ronnie Delaney. Sheila turns each idea over in her mind. Then she either nods her approval or she doesn't.

"It's gotta be something equal to what he done to Dale," I go.

"But that was an accident, Dimple."

"Right. So that's what I'm gonna make, too. A accident, see?"

Sheila gets the picture but looks worried.

"I could shove him out a window," I whisper. "Bump into him hard enough to bust the glass. It would be a accident."

Sheila looks doubtful.

I ask her, "How high would I have to be for him to get killed?"

Sheila does some quick calculating. She's a whiz at math. "At least six floors," she whispers back. "*If* he lands on cement."

"Six floors?"

"At least."

This puts a kink into my first plan, because the only building in Cuthbur with six floors is the First National Bank, and I've never been above the third, where we go to the dentist.

"Or else something with a baseball bat. But I can't make out the details of it."

Sheila squints her eyes, concentrating. "It's very tough to decapitate somebody."

Her vocabs impress me. Where does she learn 'em all?

"Too tough?"

Sheila nods.

Mama and Daddy are staring straight ahead. Their eyes are fixed like zombies on the back door of the hearse slow-rolling in front of us. They don't show any sign of hearing Sheila and me plotting against Ronnie Delaney.

"A car accident's about the only thing left," I whisper.

Sheila shakes her head. "You have to think more practically, Dimple. If you're going to plan an accident, you can't leave everything to chance."

She's got a brain and a half, I swear.

Then Sheila leans in close to me and plants a seed right in my ear. "Do you know where you could get hold of a gun?"

Suddenly I sit up straight. The idea hits me like a shot. It's perfect.

"No. Do you?"

Sheila sits silent, thinking about it. Then she goes, "Do you think Ronnie might have another one over at his house?"

If I'd thought a million years, I never could of come up with the idea of a second gun over at Ronnie's. I squeeze Sheila's hand. "Thanks."

She squeezes back.

The hearse turns in at the cemetery and crosses under a iron gate. It looks like some kind of holy horseshoe with two angels balanced at the top, both of 'em holding swords. Our Lincoln Town Car pulls through after the hearse, followed by the longest parade of mourners in Cuthbur history. All our neighbors and friends got their cars washed and shined. With those purple flags fluttering, we tie up traffic for miles.

I sure wish Dale could see it. He'd be proud.

CHAPTER EIGHT

Mr. Bert waits till everybody parks their car and walks up to the gravesite. Then he opens the back door of the hearse where Dale's coffin is. We stay in the Lincoln Town Car. My heart is beating lickety-split. My stomach feels like a rock.

I wish this burial would be a private affair with only the family coming. As it is, everybody and their brother is staring down the hill into our car.

Sheila looks out the side window. Mama and Daddy knot their fingers together. Our driver sits in the front seat like a statue. Nobody talks.

My stomach cramps worse, and I inch around to find a more comfortable position. Glancing down at my stupid dress, I suddenly remember another time I wore it. That was for the grand finale of Daily Vacation Bible School. The Baptist church had brought in this Christian magician on Saturday night to top off the week. Hosannah Houdini performed a bunch of holy tricks with sacred puppets. Like raising Lazarus from the dead, no strings attached. Like walking on the water without wetting more than his feet. Dale believed all these tricks were fake, but I couldn't say for certain.

By the end of that week, Dale and me were tied for winners of the DVBS grand prize. I won my half for reciting the Hundredth Psalm by memory. It's the one about making a joyful noise unto the Lord and entering his courts with thanksgiving. Dale won his half for reeling off the books of the Bible—clear from Genesis to Revelations—faster than Mrs. Popp, our teacher. He nailed 'em in thirty-six seconds flat, and she couldn't touch 'em in under forty.

For our reward, both of us got to ride in the backseat of Hosannah Houdini's blue Cadillac, while the magician tried to drive clear around the block of the Baptist church blindfolded. His assistant, Magic Mary, sat alongside him in the front seat giving directions. We were supposed to watch and make sure Hosannah didn't peek out of his blindfold, or Mary didn't try grabbing hold of his steering wheel. Both of us sat up on the edge of the backseat and hung over the front, keeping a close eye on 'em.

Magic Mary gave Hosannah Houdini a string of orders such as "A little to the left, duckie," and "Look out, bike rider two o'clock." He swerved some but mostly drove down the straight and narrow, like he possessed X-ray vision shining clear through that blindfold.

It came out later he had a see-through bandanna, and Magic Mary was just faking it. The *Cuthbur Examiner* printed the whole story. When Pastor Fuller found out their sin, he preached a sermon against Hosannah Houdini and Magic Mary. He announced the Baptist church was finished with magic. After that episode, Dale and me agreed to double-check all miracles before believing in any of 'em.

Stupid dress.

There's a line of chairs set on a stretch of AstroTurf right next to the grave. These are reserved for immediate family. Plus Sheila. After we're seated, Mr. Bert rolls the coffin out of the hearse, and the pallbearers heave it up the hill to where we're sitting. Danny, Screwdriver, Fitch, Robbie, Balthazar, and Nathan all belong to Dale's scout pack. It was Mama and Daddy's idea to ask 'em to be pallbearers, and it works out pretty good. All except for Fitch, who wants to trade places with Balthazar and take the middle 'cause he says he's scared of dropping his end. Truth to tell, Fitch doesn't like the feel of touching a dead boy's coffin, whether in the middle or at the end.

Straddling the top of the hole is this shiny silver

contraption with black rollers. It looks good and sturdy, kinda like a scaffold, so the coffin isn't gonna drop down by accident or ahead of schedule. Dale's casket lays on top of it, suspended in midair, while Pastor Fuller pronounces the grave words. Dale's got a blanket of black-eyed Susans, real pretty, laid over his lid. Pastor Fuller stands at the end nearest Dale's head and opens his pocket-size Bible. I know he's zeroing in on that verse about "earth to earth and ashes to ashes," like they always do in the movies.

Once he starts talking, Sheila reaches over and touches my hand. "You didn't mean it back there in the car, did you?" she whispers.

I don't show any reaction to her touch. What anybody would see if they cared to peek over at Dimple Dorfman is Rock Girl. Miss Stone-Face Supreme.

"I didn't mean *what*?" I mouth back to Sheila.

"You know," she goes, trying not to move her lips too much. "That stuff about making an 'accident' happen."

"Sure I did," I go, puckering the words out the side of my mouth like a ventriloquist.

Sheila sits silent for a minute. Maybe she's listening to Pastor Fuller's words about how we're all precious children of the Heavenly Father. That or trying to calculate how serious I am about causing a accident to happen to Ronnie Delaney. She whispers to me again, "You'd shoot him? Really?"

"Course I would." I poke a finger into her leg to display how. *Bang*.

Sheila squeezes my other hand. "Well, I wasn't serious," she goes, urging the words out from between her teeth. "I thought we were joking back there. I didn't mean it about a gun."

"That's too bad, 'cause I meant it. It's a great idea."

Sheila closes her eyes.

Daddy whispers, "Dimple," so's we cut the chatter.

"Sorry."

He's rubbing the skin off Mama's hands. Looks like it would hurt. She's got a stony smile carved into her face.

"Our departed brother Dale," Pastor Fuller is saying, "leaves a sister behind to give comfort and solace to his aggrieved parents." He swings his big head around and gives a holy nod in my direction, pointing me out to the crowd. "The little Lord Jesus, when he was just twelve years old, was already teaching the elders in the temple. Dorothea is that same age today. I pray for heaven's wisdom to . . . "

Sheez. I can*not* believe this. First the *Cuthbur Examiner* has to call me Dorothea, and now Pastor Fuller does it too. He knows good and well my name is Dimple. Didn't I say this was gonna happen? Huh?

I change channels to tune him out. I start flipping my eyes around the crowd, trying to spot if Ronnie Delaney is here. I still don't have an exact plan for the payback, but I want to get him in my sights just the same.

I see Ivy June and Mrs. Fishback hogging the front row on the other side of the casket. There's Miss Klinow, our next-door neighbor, who we call Miss Kleenex, just for a joke. And there's Mr. Roman, who works the cash register at Farm & Fleet. Strangers think his name is pronounced like "friends, Romans, and countrymen," but everybody in Cuthbur knows it's really "Ro-*mahn*."

All our family—Aunt Nell, Uncle Lucky, and such—stand lined up behind our row of chairs. The whole thing reminds me of Red Rover: townspeople versus kinfolk.

I don't see Ronnie Delaney anywhere. If he hasn't come, then that's proof positive he did it. There should be a rule, I believe: If you kill somebody, you gotta show up at the cemetery for their burial. This is plain common sense. Of course, a real murderer wouldn't follow the rules.

Now Pastor Fuller says it's time for "final com-mital." I don't recognize the last word right off, but I can tell they're about to let Dale down into the hole. Brown streamers stick out from both sides under the coffin. Mr. Bert and three of his helpers march up and grab hold of these streamers. Then the rollers on the silver contraption bend—don't ask me how—and the men muscle the coffin down into the hole. They do this real smooth and easy, like they've practiced it a lot. Hardly a bump. When Dale lands at the bottom, they tug the streamers out and move away from the hole.

Pastor Fuller steps in closer and takes charge again. Looking over at me, he goes, "Dorothea Dorfman, will you join me, please?" He holds out one hand toward me and smiles.

Everybody's looking my way, but I don't want to go stand up there next to him. Not all by myself. Daddy reaches over and nudges me on the leg. I get up and inch my way toward Pastor Fuller.

From where we're standing now, you can see clear over into the hole. Dale's coffin fills it tight from side to side. Pastor Fuller leans down and whispers into my ear, "You may throw the first handful of dirt, darling."

I never knew he wore Aqua Velva. Just like Daddy.

I whisper back to Pastor Fuller. "What's that?"

He says it again. "Now's when you throw the first handful of dirt, Dorothea."

I know what he means for me to do. I've seen this before on TV. Only nobody told me beforehand I was gonna have to do it today.

I don't move.

Pastor Fuller bends his knees and crouches down, so we're eyeball-to-eyeball. He talks to me real quiet, real gentle. "It would be a nice thing to do for your brother. But you don't have to if you don't feel like it."

I look over at Daddy, who gives me a nod.

Then I glimpse Ivy June. She's glaring at me, wishing she was the center of attention. If it was her twin brother getting buried, she'd probably pitch a whole bucketful of dirt in on him.

I bend down and pick up a single clod. I hold it in my hand, crumbling it into small pieces.

Pastor Fuller stands up straight again and says, "Of dust you were made. To dust you shall return."

Then he looks at me, and I underhand the dirt into Dale's grave. I don't throw very much, but it makes a surprising loud sound when it hits the lid of the coffin. *Bang*. A shiver shoots through me. I take a step back.

Pastor Fuller rests a hand on my shoulder. My breathing starts going faster. He nods at Mama and Daddy, who stand up and walk toward us. They bend down, pick up handfuls of dirt, and toss it in on the coffin. Their dirt makes a loud noise too. Too loud.

Our relatives line up single file. They come by, lean down, pick up dirt, and throw it in on top of Dale's coffin. *Bang. Bang.* The clods of dirt sound like gunshots exploding on the hard lid.

Sheila stands at the end of the line, but when she reaches the grave, she doesn't throw any dirt in. She just pulls out of line and stands next to me. She takes my hand.

Then all the folks on the other side of the grave line up to do the same thing. Sheila stands on one side of me. Mama and Daddy stand on the other. Both of them are crying, but they're not making any noise. Big tears roll down their cheeks. Sheila isn't crying, though. Me neither.

Miss Kleenex picks up a handful of dirt and throws it into the grave. It hits the coffin lid. *Bang.* The next person walks up and throws in more dirt. *Bang.*

Now the sound starts coming rapid-fire, shot after shot, like a repeater pistol. *Bang bang bang—*

When Ivy June marches forward, she grabs a big handful and throws it into the hole, hard. The dirt explodes on top of Dale's coffin.

That's when I break for it. I dodge around the grave and run all the way back to the Lincoln Town Car.

Sheila follows me, hurrying to catch up.

Mama and Daddy stay put where they are.

I lean against the car and fold my arms across my chest. I don't care if I get this silly dress dirty.

Sheila pulls up next to me. She's panting. She takes hold of my hand but doesn't say a word.

I stare up the hill at everybody. Mama, Daddy, Aunt Nell, Pastor Fuller. The whole stupid town. People keep turning around and looking down at me.

They start singing up at the gravesite. Pastor Fuller waves his arms up and down, keeping the people's voices together. I can hear their words clear down the hill. I lean against the biggest car in Cuthbur, standing right behind my brother's hearse, and feel my best friend's hand squeezing mine.

> *Blest be the tie that binds*
> *Our hearts in Christian love;*
> *The fellowship of kindred minds*
> *Is like to that above.*

When we asunder part,
It gives us inward pain;
But we shall still be joined in heart,
And hope to meet again.

A-men.

I turn away and try the handle of the back door. It isn't locked. "Come on, Sheila."

I climb into the Lincoln Town Car and leave the door open for her.

Sheila doesn't get in.

"I need to ride home with my mom, Dimple."

I slam the door closed and immediately regret it. I lower the window. "Sorry, Sheila."

"You've got no reason to be sorry, Dimple. I'll come over to your house tonight if I can."

I give her the best smile I can muster.

I'm inside the car by myself, but there's no pleasure left in it. All I want to do is go home now.

I look out through the window and see people starting to walk away from the gravesite.

Sheila stands next to the car for a minute. Then she moves away. I watch her head over toward Sheriff McNally.

With everybody strolling down the hill toward

their cars, I want to hide away. But there's no place to go.

I lean over and put my head between my knees.

That's when I notice this big red spot on my underwear.

What next, huh? Sheez.

CHAPTER NINE

Mama, Daddy, and me ride in the Lincoln Town Car from the cemetery back to the church. Daddy asks if I'm okay, and I tell him yeah. After that, none of us talks for the rest of the way. I appreciate this.

Once we get to the parking lot, we climb out of Mr. Bert's limo and into our old Malibu Classic. I feel like Cinderella when the clock strikes twelve. Even though her fancy carriage turned back into a pumpkin, and her fancy dress back into work clothes, I wonder was Cinderella just a little bit relieved? I know I am.

There's people galore at our house when we get home. I dash upstairs to be by myself. Mama follows as far as the doorway to my bedroom and then knocks. "Dimple?" she calls in, real quiet. "Can I come in, honey?"

I'm already pulling this stupid dress off over my head. "Come on in."

She steps inside and closes the door behind her. "Need any help?"

I yank off the dress and toss it onto the bed. "I

started my monthly back there at the cemetery," I tell her.

"Aww," Mama groans, knowing how that is. "I'll bet you didn't have anything with you, did you?"

"I wasn't expecting it, Mama."

"Of course you weren't, sweetheart. Why don't you just stay up here for a minute, okay? I'll run downstairs and get you a wet washrag and a pad from the bathroom."

"That would be nice," I tell her. "Thanks."

Mama closes the door as she goes out.

I sit down on my bed and remember the first time I got my period. It was the night Ronnie Delaney kissed me. When Dale and me got home from the Bi-County Tractor Pull, where we'd gone with Ronnie, I sat down on the toilet to relieve myself, and *whoa!*

I knew right away what was happening, of course. I'm not totally ignorant when it comes to being a girl. But I didn't have all the details down pat. Not exactly.

I yelled for Mama to come into the bathroom and help me. I remember I was so scared she might ask what I done to start it. Then I would of confessed how I let Ronnie Delaney lean over and kiss me just before the championship pull between Gonzo Gator and Big Wheel Willie.

While Mama cleaned me up that first time, she gave me a whole science lesson about why girls bleed. It surprised me because I figured it was Ronnie's kissing me caused it. Still, I can't see to this day why it's absolutely necessary. How come God made it that way? If somebody's gotta bleed in order to make babies, which is what Mama told me, then how come God said, "Let the girls do it." Huh?

Mama comes back into my room now, carrying a washrag, a mixing bowl full of warm water, and a sanitary pad.

I start cleaning up.

"Mama?"

"What, darling?"

"I'm sorry I ran away back at the cemetery. It's just that . . ."

"*Shhhh*, sweetheart." Mama takes the washrag out of my hand and rinses it in the water. "It's okay, Dimple. You did fine."

"I didn't mean no disrespect, you know."

She hushes me more. I'm trying not to cry.

"I know that. You wouldn't ever disrespect your brother, Dimple."

"But I should of . . ."

Mama takes my chin in her hand and raises my head up to look at her face. "Darling, nobody

92

blames you for running back to the car. Today was the hardest thing I ever done in my life. And it had to of been twice as hard for you."

I sniffle some.

Mama sets the bowl of water on the floor and eases herself onto the bed next to me. She puts a arm around my shoulder, and I lean into her side. Mama's always warm.

Neither of us speaks a word.

Downstairs, ladies from the Baptist church have moved in and changed our kitchen into an all-you-can-eat buffet. They're laying out a potluck as big as that time Martha's Maidens bet the tent preacher. They said they would fix two covered dishes for each soul he coaxed to come down the aisle during the last meeting of revival week. Lord, did he fool them. Preached salvation so hard you woulda thought Jesus himself was up there on the platform. "Man can't live by bread alone," the preacher shouted at us, "but he needs sweet potato pie, corn fritters, and lemon tarts too." Everybody in the canvas cathedral started laughing out loud, 'cause we knew what he was doing. Martha's Maidens complain to this day how it wasn't fair to broadcast their bet in front of heaven and hell, but the preacher said all's fair. Seventy-four souls got saved by the final tally, and Martha's Maidens had to fork over one hundred and forty-eight covered dishes to make good on their pledge come Sunday.

Dale's potluck is just about that big. There's three, four different sweet potatoes, with and without marshmallows. There's creamed corn, succotash corn, mexicali corn, and corn corn. There's lasagna, spaghetti, macaroni, and noodles with gravy. There's potato salad, potato cakes, smashed potatoes, twiced-baked, and scalloped. There's more green vegetables than down at the farmer's market on a Saturday morning, fixed with cheese sauce, bacon bits, you name it. There's hams. There's roasts. There's fried chicken. There's a turkey. And pies? Good grief, are there pies! Lemon, banana, apple, cherry, chocolate, raspberry, I can't tell you what-all. Being a pie-lover myself, I don't even bother to count how many cakes, cupcakes, and cookies there are.

The house is so full of people, they're rubbing up against each other shoulder to shoulder. I can't even see Mama or Daddy. Nobody's talking very loud. Everybody's kind of hushed.

I look around for Sheila, but I can't see her. Too many bodies. I go for the food instead. All of a sudden I feel famished. I start in with a sampler plate of banana cream pie and rhubarb pie, figuring I'll go back for the main dishes later. Then I look for a place to sit down in the living room.

All I need to do is glance at a chair, and whoever's sitting there jumps up and offers me to take their seat. That's how nice everybody's being. I choose Daddy's recliner. It's the most comfortable in the living room, and besides, it's my best lookout for who's coming in the front door. I don't think Ronnie Delaney will come to the house since he skipped the cemetery, but you can't ever be sure.

Family, friends, neighbors—just about everybody—comes over. I keep a close eye out for Ivy June and Mrs. Fishback. They're two people I don't care to talk to. If I see 'em, I'm heading the other way. So far, so good.

I know Sheila will come over. If she can.

As soon as Pastor Fuller walks into the front hall, he takes a look around the living room and spots me sitting here. He doesn't say hi to anybody else, but walks straight over to where I am.

"Dorothea?" he says. His voice is soft, almost shy.

I look up at him but can't find the right word to say back.

He crouches down, so we're face-to-face with each other. His one knee pops. Then his other one pops. They're the loudest things in the room.

"You doing okay, Dorothea?"

I got rhubarb pie in my mouth. I'm not chewing, and it's turning into paste. I nod my head and mumble, "Uh-huh."

Pastor Fuller pats me on the knee. "You're a brave girl, Dorothea. God loves you."

I try to swallow the lumpy paste of rhubarb.

He keeps talking. Everybody else in the room is hushed up so they can hear what's he's telling me. "You believe in eternal life, don't you, Dorothea?"

I close my eyes and order my throat to swallow.

"Dale's up in heaven. It's like the Bible says . . ."

In one big gulp, I manage to down the rhubarb. Then I have to pucker a few times to wash out all the juice.

". . . he who believes in me will not perish."

Finally I can talk, and I say, *Dimple!* But I choke on the word, so he can't make it out.

"What?" Pastor Fuller asks.

"Dimple," I say again, clearer this time. "My name's Dimple, not Dorothea."

Pastor Fuller stops talking. He looks confused.

"You keep calling me Dorothea, but you know my name's Dimple."

"In the Lamb's Book of Life, every name is recorded as it—"

I butt in without meaning to be rude. "In the Lamb's Book of Life, my name is Dimple. Not Dorothea."

Pastor Fuller pauses and tries to take in this information. To his way of thinking, the Lamb's Book of Life requires official names. Like on your birth certificate. Like on a driver's license. I can tell he's having a hard time accepting the idea of a nickname. He wouldn't want me to miss out on heaven by mistaken identity.

Pastor Fuller stands up. His knees don't pop this time, but he groans with the effort of it.

"You're probably right. If His eye is on the sparrow, I expect the good Lord can remember 'Dimple.' Still, there's nothing wrong with 'Dorothea,' you know."

I look up at him and nod. Inside, I'm not worrying about if it's "Dorothea" or "Dimple" printed in the Lamb's Book of Life. After I even the score with Ronnie Delaney, my name ain't gonna be there any way you look at it.

By the time Ronnie's folks arrive, most everybody's stuffed. Sheila is here, and we're sitting on the stairs together. I'm looking down into a half plate of scalloped potatoes. I can't say why I keep going back for more helpings. Maybe I just like

97

the sound of "Here, Dimple, you can go in front of us, honey."

Mr. and Mrs. Delaney knock soft on our front door, so nobody hears 'em at first.

Finally, somebody from the living room hollers, "Come on in. Door's open."

I heft myself up and go open the door.

They're not expecting to see me, I can tell. Both Ronnie's parents look sheepish standing there, and I feel sorry for 'em. "Come on in," I go.

"We won't stay but a minute," Mr. Delaney says. "We just wanted to pay our respects to your mama and daddy."

I nod and move outta their way. "There's gobs of food," I tell 'em.

Mrs. Delaney is like, "We won't be eating. We only want to see your folks." She's talking real soft. "And you, too, Dimple."

I got no bone to pick with Ronnie's folks. After all, they aren't the ones who shot Dale. I try to look friendly.

Mr. Delaney goes, "There just aren't any words for how sorry we feel, Dimple. We thought the world of your brother, you know."

"Uh-huh."

Mrs. Delaney reaches a hand out and touches me on the shoulder.

"Where's Ronnie?" I go, making the question sound like it's by-the-way.

Mr. and Mrs. Delaney look at each other before answering me. Then he says, "Ronnie's at home. He didn't think he'd be welcome here tonight."

"He knows how you must feel, Dimple," Mrs. Delaney explains. "We all do."

I don't say anything to this. I just repeat, "Why don't you go get yourself some food?"

"We won't be staying that long," Mr. Delaney says.

I flatten myself up against the stairs so they can squeeze past and go down the hall toward the kitchen. They already told me all I need to know. So, Ronnie's home alone, is he?

I tell Sheila I gotta be by myself for a while and push past her to go up to my bedroom. She eyes me kinda funny but doesn't say anything. I don't stop to wonder what she must be thinking. All I concentrate on is: Now's the time.

Never delay a payback.

CHAPTER TEN

It's easy for me to climb out my bedroom window, jump to the front porch roof, hang from the drainpipe, then drop to the ground below. Dale and me do it all the time.

The Delaneys live just two blocks away from our house. It's dark outside, and I gotta hurry. No telling how long I'll have before somebody comes looking for me. Along the street, there's cars parked most all the way there. Some still got purple funeral flags hooked onto their radio antennas. I cross into the grass and start stripping pennants off the cars, collecting souvenirs. I get eleven of 'em before spotting Ronnie's house. It stands in the middle of the next block.

I balance on the curb for a minute, teetering, looking down toward their place. There's only one window lit in the whole house so far as I can see, and that's upstairs. Ronnie has got to be up there, on the second story. Or else he's sitting somewhere in the dark, which doesn't seem likely. I've never been upstairs at the Delaneys' house before. Upstairs is reserved for Ronnie and Dale. Whenever the three of us play together, we do it in their living room, or else downstairs in their basement.

I walk along the curb pretending like it's a tightrope, clear to the end of the block. At the corner, I step into the street and kneel down beside a storm drain. I take all the purple flags I've collected and fold 'em in half, two at a time. Then I stuff 'em through the iron grate. They only make a teeny sound when they hit the water, and then they float away underground. While stuffing the storm drain, I peer up the half block to Ronnie's house. Right next door, I can see Ivy June's. They've got all their lights blazing, of course—every single one of 'em. I look back at the single light in the upstairs window at the Delaneys and repeat to myself: Ronnie's got to be in there.

I stand up, brush off the knees of my jeans, and start walking slowly down the block. I keep to the street instead of getting back up on the curb or on the sidewalk. It hits me all of a sudden that I'm taking the same route Dale walked through Cuthbur on the night he died. Only he didn't walk it, I bet. He ran it. All the way from our house, down the street, clear to Ronnie's. He had a good reason to run—a reason which I know, and he knows, but nobody else does.

It was to get away from me.

In the middle of the block, I stop. I'm standing on the street right in front of the Delaneys' yard. There's still just the one light on upstairs. The curtain is drawn, and I can't see inside. Next door, Ivy June's house is blazing with wasted electricity. I step over the curb, creep into the shadow of a thick maple tree, and let my back slide down its trunk till I'm sitting on the cool grass. I want to think some things out before making my next move.

The day before Dale died, me and him had this big argument. It started during a TP club meeting in the part called New Business. Dale made a motion that when we grow up we should live together and keep on being Twin Protectors forever and ever. But I said I didn't think I would second that. I felt like we oughta table it, which is club talk for thinking it over some more before voting. He wanted to know how come, and I said I hadn't made up my mind for sure if I was gonna get married or not.

As the President of TP, Dale declared I could take exactly three minutes then and there to make up my mind if I was going to get married someday. I told him I didn't think that was long enough to decide such a thing. Besides, nobody had asked me to marry them yet, and that complicated things.

Dale wanted to know if I had somebody in mind for a husband. I fibbed and went, "No, I don't, but maybe somebody'll come along. You never know."

Then Dale looked at his watch and called for the answer to his question, meaning time was up.

I told him I didn't want to vote right then.

And he said, "Who's President here, anyway?"

Then I said, "Just wait till the next election, butthead."

Dale couldn't believe the way our Social Director was smarting off to our President. He said we might as well break up Twin Protectors right then if I couldn't show any more respect for the office of President than to call him a butthead. Besides, he said, who wanted me in the club anyhow, if I was gonna run off and get married someday.

I told him that was about the stupidest thing I ever heard him say. I had no plans to run away and get married. On top of that, he was living proof that buttheads can talk.

He told me to shut my big mouth. As far as Dale was concerned, Twin Protectors was officially dead, and I'd killed it by considering getting married.

I told him, "Fine with me. Who needs this stupid club anyway?"

He said, "Well, I sure don't."

And I said, "Me neither, buster."

And he said, "Fine."

And I said, *"Fine!"*

And that was that.

I stand up. My bottom's beginning to get damp from the dew on the grass. I'm thinking Dale and me woulda patched things over if we got the chance. I know we would of. We always did before. Besides, I'm thinking, did we ever take a vote on ending Twin Protectors? No, we did not. There was not one single word recorded in the minutes. Not even "butthead." The way I see it, TP is still alive and kicking. Now I aim to prove it.

I study the Delaneys' house, calculating the best place to break and enter. It doesn't make sense to go in by their front door. The staircase leading up to the second story is right inside there, and I don't want Ronnie to hear me coming. So I decide to sneak around back instead. Go in through the kitchen.

Nobody in Cuthbur locks a door. Not the front or the back. Neighbors expect to walk right in and holler, "Anybody home?" If someone *was* to lock their door, neighbors might figure they had something to hide or were up to no good. They'd start talking, filling in the blanks. In Cuthbur, a open-door policy is a person's best protection.

I step onto the Delaneys' front lawn, and a chill of remembering runs up my legs.

I didn't sleep one wink that night Dale and me argued, the last night he was alive. I remember I laid upstairs in my bed thinking everything through. I just about changed my mind and decided not to get married after all, no matter who asked me. I figured Dale was a lot more fun than any other boy in Cuthbur could be, so why not just live with him for the rest of my life? Besides, when we growed up, Twin Protectors could have a million adventures together.

I consider walking around the Delaneys' house on the left side, next to the Sosas'. Only they don't have any lights on at all, and I don't like things to be *too* dark. So I head along the right side instead, edging up close to the bushes, keeping out of sight of the snoopy Fishbacks.

I sneak with my back squeezed next to the Delaneys' house and my eyes facing toward the Fishbacks'. When I'm halfway to the back, I spy Ivy June sitting at their dining-room table. I hit the dirt. From ground level, I can't spot Mrs. Fishback in the picture anywhere. Thank goodness Ivy June doesn't look up from whatever she's doing. Probably cutting fashion models outta magazines, knowing her. I get on my hands and knees and crawl the rest of the way around to the back, quiet as a thief in the night.

The Delaneys got a screen door in front of the big wooden one leading into their kitchen. It squeaks when I pull it open. I freeze for an instant, standing there like a statue, to make sure nobody's coming. All except for my brain, which is whizzing around inside my head a thousand miles an hour.

I had decided to tell Dale first thing that next morning how I changed my mind and wasn't gonna get married after all. But then I saw the mood he was in at the breakfast table and knew I better wait. If I told him right then, he probably woulda gone, "Forget it, sister. It's too late now. Go on and get married, if that's what you want. I knew you'd turn out to be a girl in the end." Sheez, the things I gotta put up with as TP Social Director.

The knob on the Delaneys' kitchen door turns easy when I try it. I slide inside their house smooth as smoke and close the door behind me. I stand quiet for a minute, getting used to the darkness. A little window over the sink looks out toward the Fishbacks' house and borrows some of their light. I think about Ronnie's mother having to do dishes and catching glimpses of Ivy June all the time. I feel sorry for her.

As soon as I get my bearings, I start to see

shadows marking where the kitchen table is and where Mrs. Delaney's ironing board stands, stacked high with pressing. I begin moving around the kitchen, tender-footed and slow. I can't hear any sound through the whole house, except for the ghost-shuffling of my own feet.

I think again: Ronnie has got to be upstairs someplace.

In my mind, I'm wondering where the Delaneys might keep another gun. If they have another gun.

Time's pushing me, and I got to keep moving. But I don't want to make a mistake and overlook some detail. I inch along the kitchen cabinets and pull open all the drawers as I go.

Silverware.

Dish towels.

Measuring cups and wooden spoons.

I don't believe anybody would keep a gun in a drawer with their cookie cutters, but you can't be sure. It pays to check.

Under the sink, next to the dish soap, I find a roll of gray duct tape and pick that up, sliding it over my right wrist like a big bracelet. It might come in handy.

While I'm searching, I can't stop my brain from thinking about Dale. When I told him I didn't know who I wanted to marry, that was not completely true. If he'd put me under oath and made me speak the whole truth and nothing but the truth, I'd of had to say I did know.

I would of spoke the name Ronnie Delaney.

I admit Ronnie and me have never actually talked about getting married. Heck, he doesn't even know I like him. Liked him. It just made sense to me he would be the one, that's all. With him and Dale already best friends, I figured marrying Ronnie would be like adding a new member to the club. Twin Protectors Plus One.

If I'd confessed this to Dale, he would of laughed to kingdom come. You better believe he would of. Fact is, he probably would of come straight over here to Ronnie's house and told *him*. Then where would I be, huh?

From the kitchen I go into the Delaneys' dining room. A streak of street light comes through the front window, so I can see pretty good. On a hunch, I go down on all fours and crawl under the table, reaching my hand up. I feel around the end where Mr. Delaney sits. It could be he keeps a gun stashed under here just in case somebody breaks in while they're eating Sunday dinner.

I feel wooden bumps now and again, screw holes, and a piece of petrified chewing gum.

No gun.

Bad luck.

I bump my back against the tabletop when I stand up.

The Delaneys got a dining-room hutch along the wall that holds all their china. I walk up to it and grab hold of the pulls on the drawer. It slides good even though the silverware inside is heavy. When I feel around, I clink some of the knives and forks together. I freeze for fear of rousing Ronnie's suspicion upstairs. I wouldn't want to give up the element of surprise.

Thinking of Ronnie kicks me back into that other thing. Twin Protectors Plus One. Things mighta worked out. You never can tell. It wasn't like Dale and me would of let him run for office or anything. He would of just been a regular, dues-paying member with a few honorary privileges.

Spilled milk now. No use crying over it.

From the dining room I walk into the front hall and stand at the bottom of the stairs. I debate whether to go up right away or cross over into the living room first. I bend my right arm at the elbow so the roll of duct tape won't slip off. There *could* be a gun in the living room. But I decide I can't take the time to look for it now. I'm pressing my luck as it is. I need to go straight upstairs.

I take the steps real cautious, one at a time, letting my weight ease down and testing for creaks.

As I get toward the top, I peer over the railing and look around. Like I told you, I've never been up here before. Two doors are visible at the end of the hall where the stairs land. Both are open, but they got no lights on. At the very top of the steps, I turn and look the opposite way. Clear at the other end of the hall, facing out toward the street, is a third room. The door to it is half open and the light's lit.

That's gotta be where Ronnie is.

I start walking down the hall real quiet—one step, one step—toward the doorway. The Delaneys got thick carpet, and I don't make a single noise as I walk. He's got the TV on in there with the sound turned down low. I can't tell what show he's watching. No way Ronnie can hear me coming, that's for sure.

I stop next to the doorway. I lean up against the wall so I won't cast any shadow into the room. I slip the roll of duct tape off my wrist and dig my fingernails into it to peel back a strip. I do it slow so there's no ripping sound when the tape comes unwound. As soon as I get about one foot of tape stretched out between my hands, I take a step closer to the door.

Life can be strange. Just three days ago, I planned on marrying Ronnie Delaney, my twin brother's best friend. Now Dale is dead, and I plan on shooting Ronnie Delaney instead.

That is, if I can find a gun to do it with.

I don't have any plan of action but just follow my gut. I blast into the room with duct tape cocked.

"DON'T MOVE A MUSCLE, SUCKER!" I scream at Ronnie. "NOT IF YOU WANT TO LIVE ANOTHER TEN SECONDS!"

CHAPTER ELEVEN

Ronnie is sitting in a wooden chair that matches the ones in the dining room downstairs. His back is to the door. He jerks around to see who's there, looking surprised as heck. As soon as he recognizes it's me, he knows I mean business. "Don't do anything, Dimple," he goes.

"SHUT UP!" I scream. "YOU SHUT UP!"

I jump around to the front of his chair and land on both my feet. I face him nose-to-nose, raging like a demon. I turn and snap off his TV, then wheel back again. I stretch out my duct tape and press it tight across his lips and cheeks. "I TOLD YOU TO SHUT UP, DIDN'T I?" I yell at him, flattening the tape down hard.

Ronnie doesn't make any effort to resist or talk. Good thing, too. He pops his eyes wide open. He's staring into mine, watching for what I'm gonna do next. I rip the tape off the roll.

"HANDS BEHIND YOUR BACK!" My voice is stuck on blaster volume.

His eyes look like a rabbit's just before you conk it on the head with your baseball bat.

I scream at him again. "PUT YOUR HANDS BEHIND YOUR BACK!"

He does what I tell him and pulls both his arms behind the chair. I run around to the other side, dig my fingers into the tape, and tear off a long piece. "DON'T MOVE," I holler. "PUT YOUR HANDS TOGETHER."

I wrap the duct tape around and around his wrists, pulling it as tight as I can, and then rip off the end. I slide up his arms and wrap another two loops around his elbows.

Ronnie lets out a little groan.

"YOU THINK I WON'T DO IT TO YOU LIKE YOU DONE IT TO DALE, DON'T YOU?"

He's too scared to shake his head.

"JUST BECAUSE WE'RE FRIENDS. AT LEAST I *THOUGHT* WE WERE FRIENDS."

Ronnie tries wiggling free, but he can't move. I've got him pinned down good.

"WELL, I WILL," I rage at him. "I WILL IF I HAVE TO."

I walk back around to the front of him. It feels good to be screaming. "YOU GONNA MOVE NOW?"

Ronnie shakes his head no.

"DON'T THINK I'M GONNA TRUST YOU. I'M NOT. NOT FOR ONE SECOND."

I bend over and begin taping one of his ankles to the chair leg. "NOT AFTER WHAT YOU DONE TO DALE!"

I wrap it good and tight, five times around, and then tear it off the roll. "YOU'VE GOTTA PAY, RONNIE DELANEY. IF I DON'T GET SOME STRAIGHT ANSWERS ABOUT MY BROTHER, YOU'RE GONNA PAY THE SAME WAY DALE DID. YES, SIR."

I inch over and tape his other leg to the chair. Then I stand up.

Ronnie can't move at all now. Except maybe to wet his pants. His mouth is taped shut. His hands and arms are wrapped behind his back. His legs are fixed to the chair.

"HOW YOU FEELING?" I scream at him, leaning in close to his face. "IS THIS HOW YOU DONE IT TO DALE? DID YOU TIE HIM UP FIRST?"

Ronnie doesn't move a muscle.

"HUH?"

His eyes look like they wanta cry, but he's too scared to turn on the water.

"NOT MUCH FUN, IS IT?"

Ronnie closes his eyelids.

"OPEN YOUR EYES," I scream. "LOOK AT ME, YOU HEAR?"

He opens 'em back up and looks at me.

"YOU GOTTA *SEE* WHAT I'M GONNA DO TO YOU."

Ronnie starts sucking air, breathing . . . in . . . out . . . in . . . out. His chest heaves.

"DIDN'T I TELL YOU NOT TO MOVE?" I scream at him.

He squints his eyes to keep from crying. But he can't stop now.

"DALE DIDN'T CRY. MY BROTHER DIDN'T CRY. I CAN GUARANTEE YOU THAT."

Ronnie tries closing his eyes again to stop the tears. Then he opens 'em back up and takes one quick glance away from my face toward the front window. I follow along and notice how the window's open an inch at the bottom. I walk over there in three big steps, grab hold at the top, and shove the window down hard. I lock the latch.

"NOBODY'S COMING TO YOUR RESCUE, MISTER. FORGET IT."

Ronnie stops himself from crying somehow.

"DID ANYBODY COME TO DALE'S RESCUE? HUH? DID THEY?"

I can feel my own breathing race faster and faster. My chest is pounding. I sit down on the floor in front of Ronnie. I hold what's left of the duct tape in both my hands, like a weapon.

"I gotta think," I say, surprised to hear my voice

isn't screaming anymore.

Ronnie keeps his eyes glued to mine. He looks like a murderer strapped into the electric chair.

I take a deep breath, trying to slow down my heaving chest. Think. Think.

"Is this where you did it to Dale?" I ask Ronnie.

He doesn't try to answer me. Doesn't move a muscle.

"IS THIS WHERE YOU KILLED DALE?"

He shakes his head from side to side.

"ANSWER ME."

He closes his eyes, then opens 'em again right away.

I stand up and start to pace the room. I walk to the front window, back to Ronnie's chair, then back to the window again. I can see down into the street where a line of cars is still parked for our funeral potluck. I can't say for certain how long it's been since I left the house. I've lost track of time. I pace back to Ronnie.

"Okay," I go. "I'm gonna take your mouth tape off. But if you let out so much as one PEEP, I'm gonna do you in right here and now. YOU UNDER-STAND?"

Ronnie nods his head yes.

I take hold of one end of the duct tape and rip it from left to right across his cheeks and lips. A wide red mark appears clear across his face from where the tape pinches and tears at his skin. Musta hurt plenty, but Ronnie doesn't cry out. I wouldn't marry no chicken.

I point a finger into his face. "NOW YOU'RE GONNA TALK, MISTER. I DON'T HAVE TIME TO PLAY NO GAMES OF CLUE. YOU'RE GONNA TELL ME EVERYTHING I NEED TO KNOW AND TELL IT TO ME NOW. THEN I PROMISE I'LL FINISH THE JOB QUICK."

Ronnie doesn't move. Smart of him.

"THE FIRST THING," I go, keeping my finger aimed straight between his eyes. "WHERE DID YOU DO IT TO DALE?"

Ronnie shakes his head.

"TALK TO ME, BOY."

"No," he says, sounding so quiet I can barely hear him.

"SPEAK UP."

"No," he repeats a little louder.

"WHAT DO YOU MEAN, *NO*?" I scream.

Ronnie closes his eyes.

"YOU GOTTA TELL ME WHAT HAPPENED HERE. IT'S *MY* STORY, AND YOU'RE GONNA GIVE IT TO ME. NOBODY ELSE WILL."

Ronnie lets out a deep breath but doesn't say anything.

I look around the room, taking mental note of all the furniture. There's a double bed, a half dresser with a mirror above it, and a long chest of drawers behind me where the TV sits.

"IS THIS YOUR FOLKS' ROOM?"

Ronnie nods.

I lower my pointer finger, tap my chin, and try to think. I can feel Ronnie's eyes digging into me. I can hear a clock ticking from somewhere. That or my heart beating.

"WHERE'S *YOUR* ROOM?"

Ronnie turns his head in the direction of the hallway.

"TALK TO ME!"

When he speaks, his voice comes out kinda creaky. "First door on the right," he says.

I stare down the dark hallway. My heart is banging away inside my chest. If I have to do it to Ronnie, it's gotta be in the same room where he done it to Dale. But I can't risk letting him loose.

Suddenly, the solution comes to me outta the blue.

I lean down and put my face right next to his. This time I whisper instead of screaming. But he can still hear me; don't you worry.

"Where's the gun, Ronnie?"

He lets his eyes droop closed, like this was the

one question he was afraid I might ask. Ronnie is getting the picture of just how serious I am.

I grab his chin in my right hand and whisper to him again. "Tell me where the gun is, Ronnie."

"The police took it," he goes, mumbling his words on account of my tight grip.

"THE *OTHER* ONE," I scream, shooting a threatening tone through my voice. All of a sudden, I'm dead certain there has to be another gun.

Ronnie gets a scared look in his eyes, worse than before.

Bingo. There's another gun, all right.

"WHERE IS IT?"

He won't answer me.

I grab hold of both his shoulders. "WHERE'S THE DARN GUN? WE DON'T HAVE ALL NIGHT, AND I KNOW IT'S HERE SOMEPLACE."

"Please, Dimple," Ronnie goes. "I didn't shoot him."

I let go of his shoulders and fall back two steps. It's like his words give me a hard shove right in the chest.

"DON'T YOU LIE TO ME, RONNIE DELANEY," I scream at him. "IF YOU'RE LYING TO ME, I WON'T NEED A GUN TO DO THE JOB. YOU HEAR ME?"

"I'm not lying to you, Dimple. You can believe

what you want. But the truth is Dale shot himself."

"LIAR!" I step forward. I want to slap Ronnie, but I don't do it. "YOU'RE LYING TO ME."

"I was here with him," Ronnie goes, his voice getting stronger. "You weren't here, were you? I know what happened, and you don't."

"SHUT UP, CREEP!"

"If you want to know the truth, I'm the only one who can tell you."

"I SAID TO SHUT UP!"

"Then make up whatever story you want to, Dimple. I thought you liked to get things right."

"QUIET," I scream.

I need quiet for a minute. I need time to think. Details are beginning to get confused in my brain.

But I can't find quiet. Not enough of it. The clock keeps ticking. My chest keeps banging. There's not enough time to think.

My voice hurts, but I keep on screaming. "THE PAPER SAID YOU FOUND A GUN UNDER THE MATTRESS."

Ronnie doesn't say anything. He keeps his eyes on me.

"WAS IT *THIS* MATTRESS?"

I walk around behind Ronnie to his parents' bed. I yank back the spread, throw one pillow to the ground, then lean over and grab the other pillow.

"ANSWER ME! DID YOU FIND THE GUN IN THIS ROOM?"

Ronnie nods his head without twisting around to look at me.

I slide a hand in under the sheet and feel. Then I drop down on my knees and push my whole arm in between the mattress and the box spring. "IS THIS WHERE YOU FOUND IT?"

He doesn't answer.

I don't feel any gun in there. But somehow I know I'm getting close.

I pull my arm back out and stand up. Ronnie's taped tight to the chair, so I know he won't move. I walk around to the other side of the bed. I jerk the spread all the way off onto the floor. This time I don't bother to feel under the sheet. If there's a gun, it's gotta be under the mattress, I just know it. I kneel down and shove both hands into the crease. Anybody looking at me might think I was praying: "Now I lay me down to sleep."

I make a wide sweeping motion with both my arms but don't feel a thing. I can't believe it. Something inside me is dead certain there's another gun in this room. If Ronnie and Dale found theirs on the other side of the bed, then I'm gonna find mine on this side.

I pull my arms out and walk on my knees closer

to the headboard. I push in again under the mattress, this time using just my right arm. I'm in clear up to my shoulder, stretching out my fingers and squinting my eyes for extra push. Then suddenly, right when I'm ready to give up the search, I touch something.

Oh my goodness.

"What have we here?" I go, opening my eyes and looking over at the back of Ronnie's head. "It feels cold. It feels hard. I wonder what it could be?"

I pull the gun out from under the mattress and stand there looking at it. I feel like Hosannah Houdini. Shocked by the success of his own trick.

"Got any ideas, Ronnie?" I ask him.

The gun's heavier than you might think. Heavier than it looks.

"Is this a .22 caliber?" I ask him.

But Ronnie's not talking. His head slumps forward.

I don't have time for games.

"LET'S GET THIS OVER WITH," I scream. "IT'S MY LAST PAYBACK, AND I DON'T AIM TO DELAY IT!"

CHAPTER TWELVE

I've never handled a gun before. But I've seen enough of 'em on TV to know how to work one.

"DON'T TRY ANYTHING FUNNY," I scream at Ronnie.

I'm trying to unwrap his ankles with my left hand while holding the gun in my right. Duct tape sticks good. You've got to pull it off just right, and I'm in a hurry.

"STOP MOVING. YOU HEAR ME?"

"I'm not moving." All the umph has drained out of Ronnie's voice.

I keep struggling with the stupid tape. Finally it loosens enough for him to wriggle one foot out.

"Okay now," I warn him. "I'm gonna undo your hands, but I got this GUN aimed straight at your head, so you can just FORGET ABOUT messing with me."

Ronnie doesn't say anything. He knows I mean business.

I untape his elbows next, then his hands. They're red and raw, like his face. He brings his arms around front real slow and starts rubbing his wrists together.

I'm standing about three feet away, facing him, holding the gun. "You can undo that other foot yourself," I order.

Ronnie leans down. He keeps looking up to check my trigger finger.

"MOVE IT!"

He tugs at the tape and manages to twist it back on itself.

"WE DON'T GOT ALL NIGHT."

Ronnie works at unsticking the tape. He doesn't risk saying a word back to me.

When he gets his other foot loose from the chair, I tell him, "GET UP!"

He stands up.

"ALL RIGHT NOW."

The gun's beginning to feel more comfortable in my hand.

"YOU SHOW ME WHERE DALE GOT HIS."

I wag the gun at him when I talk.

"I'M FOLLOWING RIGHT BEHIND YOU. HEAR?"

He starts walking toward the door. I'm not stupid enough to stick the gun right in his back where he could turn around and grab it. I hold it a couple feet away. Still, I know he can feel it there.

Ronnie steps down the hallway. The only light

to see by comes from behind my back, from Mr. and Mrs. Delaney's bedroom.

He turns in at the first door on the right.

"HOLD IT." I hear my voice echo down the open space. "Reach in along the wall, REAL SLOW, and turn on the light."

He lifts his right arm, snakes his hand around the edge of the door, and feels for the switch. Ronnie's wrist is chapped and scraped from where the duct tape stuck to his skin.

The light flicks on.

"INSIDE!" I order him.

He inches into his own bedroom with suspicion, like he's afraid of what might be in there.

"GO ON."

He won't speed up. Isn't in any hurry.

"MOVE IT."

Once inside the room, I tell Ronnie to lie down on his bed spread-eagled.

He seems confused by what I mean.

"FACEDOWN. ARMS AND LEGS APART."

Now he does it.

I keep the gun pointed at him while I walk around the room. To the left side of the bed. To the right.

All of a sudden, I stop. I spot a huge bloodstain on the floor. It's on the right side of his bed.

"LIFT UP YOUR HEAD AND LOOK OVER HERE."

Ronnie doesn't follow my order. He keeps his face buried in the bed covers, shaking his head no, no. He doesn't want to see anything.

"I SAID TO LOOK OVER HERE."

He keeps shaking his head. He says something, but I can't make out the words.

"LIFT UP YOUR HEAD, DARN IT. I CAN'T HEAR YOU."

Ronnie raises his face up just enough to talk. He still refuses to look at where I'm pointing.

"Shoot me," he says.

"WHAT? WHAT DID YOU SAY?"

"Shoot me."

I don't answer this. Sheez. Who's the one giving orders around here?

On the tan carpet, between his bed and his dresser, is a stain the shape of the Great Lakes. The color is somewhere between red and brown. It's almost purple. I know it's Dale's blood I'm looking at, soaked into the carpet from the shooting.

I want Ronnie to look at it. I want him to tell me what I already know.

"IS THIS WHERE YOU DID IT TO HIM?"

Ronnie's face is buried back in the covers

again. His shoulders are shaking, but I don't hear any bawling.

I kneel down on the floor and press my hand into the bloodstain. Gently at first. Then harder. It feels stiff.

Sheez, what did I expect? Did I think it was gonna be wet? I can be so stupid sometimes.

I stand up again and walk over to the dresser, making sure I don't step on any of the blood. There's a TV sitting there, with Super Nintendo alongside of it.

"SIT UP!"

Ronnie shakes his head. He doesn't want to sit up.

"I AIN'T GONNA SHOOT YOU IN THE BACK."

Still, he doesn't move.

"Come on now. Sit up, Ronnie."

I want him to look at me. I need him to look at me. It's beginning to feel creepy being the only one noticing all this blood.

I tell him, "You don't have to look at the floor if you don't want to, Ronnie."

With that, he starts to move a little on the bed. Real slow, he sits up, pulling his legs underneath him, facing away from the dresser with the TV and the Super Nintendo. He stares straight out the doorway.

"Over here, Ronnie. I'm over here."

But he doesn't look in my direction.

"The blood's all dried, you know. It can't hurt you now."

I don't know what makes me say this. I'm beginning to feel a little sorry for him, seeing how upset he is. I've never known Ronnie Delaney to be scared of anything before. And that includes me.

Ronnie's eyes are closed.

"For crying out loud," I say. "How do you sleep in here at night?"

He doesn't answer me.

"Huh? How do you sleep in here if you're so afraid?"

He whispers, "I don't."

I can barely hear him. "What did you say?"

"I don't sleep in here."

"Why not? This is your room, isn't it?"

"I sleep in *their* room."

"Whose? Your folks'? You sleep with them?"

Ronnie nods his head, but he's still got his eyes closed. Have you ever noticed how hard it is to talk to somebody when they got their eyes closed?

"I haven't slept in here since it happened."

I step across the bloodstain and walk over to the doorway so he can look up and see me without getting sick.

"Open your stupid eyes. I wanta look at you, Ronnie."

He opens 'em very slow and glances up at me. I'm holding the gun with both my hands and pointing it at him. In the back of my mind I keep hearing the motto from Twin Protectors repeated over and over: "Never delay a payback." But for some reason I'm in no hurry. There's one or two details I need to find out before I shoot him.

"Ronnie?" I say. "What happened in here on Saturday night? Just tell me the truth, and don't lie to me."

He shakes his head and goes, "When have I ever lied to you, Dimple?"

I'm beginning to feel confused, like he's getting the upper hand. I can't let that happen.

"Talk, then," I tell him. "I'm listening."

Ronnie sits up straighter. He keeps his eyes locked on me, or else they might slip over and see Dale's bloodstain. "It was an accident," he goes. "An awful accident."

"I said for you to tell me *what* happened. I'll be the judge of what's a accident and what's on purpose."

Ronnie nods his head.

I let go of the gun with my left hand and hold it in my right. My arms are getting tired. I don't see how a hostage taker keeps up his strength for holding the gun so long.

Ronnie tries to concentrate on remembering. "It was all my fault," he says. "We were playing 'Street Justice' on Super Nintendo. Dale had never played it before, and he wanted to try it out."

I listen close for the details of what he's saying. That's where I can sniff out a lie if he's telling one.

"Dale liked the game, but he said the graphics weren't true."

"What do you mean they weren't true?"

"Dale said the guns were too small. They didn't look right."

"Hmmm."

I consider this. I never played "Street Justice" myself. I didn't even know Ronnie had it. The game just came out. Dale and me read about it in a magazine, and I remember it got a B+ rating.

Ronnie keeps going. "I told Dale they do research on this stuff at the factory, and they're not going to make a mistake with their graphics."

"What did Dale say to that?"

"He still said the guns looked too small. Like he was an expert or something. He said they didn't look realistic to him."

I nod my head when I hear this, knowing how stubborn my brother can be. He hates to admit when he doesn't know something.

"So I told him, if you're so darn smart, you tell me what type of gun a street fighter uses."

I nod again.

"And Dale told me it sure wouldn't be any little popgun like they show in the graphics of this game."

Hearing the word "popgun" gets to me. Ronnie must be telling me the truth so far, because that's exactly what Dale would of said.

"What happened next?" I ask him. "Hurry up and get to the part where you shoot him."

Ronnie looks down at the bedspread. Then he looks right back up at me. It's like he doesn't want to go on anymore.

I'm beginning to get nervous myself. He's coming to the end, and I know how everything turns out. Still, whatever happened to Dale is *my* story, and I've got to hear it all.

My right arm is getting dead tired. I bring my left hand back up to steady the gun and then bend both my arms at the elbows to ease the strain.

Ronnie starts talking again without me prompting him. "I never should have told Dale about the gun," he goes in a quiet voice.

It's like Ronnie is talking to himself now instead of to me.

"I should of kept my stupid mouth shut. I

should of just said, 'You're right, Dale. You're always right, Dale. Those graphics are unrealistic. Those guns are too small.' "

"Don't tell me what you should of done. Tell me what you done."

Ronnie nods his head. He keeps going. I can tell he's seeing the details of what happened next as he speaks 'em.

"I was mad at Dale for being such a know-it-all. I told him he was an idiot jerkface."

"Dale? You told Dale he was a idiot jerkface?"

"Yeah."

This story is making me feel antsy. I need to get to the end of it fast. Nobody calls my brother a idiot jerkface and gets away with it.

I pull back the hammer, *click*, and cock my gun. Just like on TV.

Ronnie's eyes stare straight at me, but they don't seem focused. It's like he's looking at somebody else holding the gun and not at me.

"I told Dale he didn't know squat about guns," Ronnie goes. "And he said he knew a heck of a lot more about guns than I did."

The gun in my sweaty hands is starting to feel too heavy to hold up anymore. I almost drop it.

I glance down at the cocked lever, and I finger the trigger.

Ronnie keeps pushing ahead toward the end of his story.

"So I went into my parents' room and got the gun out from under my dad's side of the mattress. I brought it back in here to show Dale."

"Was it just like this one?"

"Exactly like that one," Ronnie says. "They're matching .22 calibers. One for my mom and one for my dad. A pistol on each side of their bed. For protection."

My hands begin to shake. How could a measly .22 weigh so much? Sheez, a .22 is nothing more than a popgun, Dale told me.

Ronnie's ready to finish the story now, and I couldn't stop him if I wanted to. "So I handed him the gun," he goes.

"You handed it to Dale?"

"Yes. And I told him to be careful because it was loaded."

My palms are sweating. My trigger finger twitches.

"Dale tossed the gun up in the air and caught it. He was playing like it was a toy gun. I said for him to stop it, but he wouldn't."

I can see the whole scene as Ronnie's talking. I know he's not lying to me now because it's so easy to see.

"Dale was laughing real loud like he does sometimes. You know what I mean?"

I nod, hearing exactly which laugh he's talking about.

"Then he stretched his arm way out . . ."

Ronnie lifts his own arm to show me how it happened.

"Dale pointed the pistol back at himself, and . . ."

Ronnie can't go on anymore. He lowers his head into his hands and cries, "It was my fault, Dimple. It was all my fault."

I take a step toward Ronnie. I want to tell him it *wasn't* his fault. Not really.

But when I move forward, a drop of sweat drips into my right eye. It stings. I reach up to wipe it out.

And that's when I squeeze the trigger.

CHAPTER THIRTEEN

The shot from the pistol echoes in my head. This little .22 makes a bigger pop than you've ever heard in your life. My ears hurt. My arms hurt. They ache. But I don't care. Ronnie is what matters. Did I kill him?

I place the gun on the floor and run toward the bed.

Ronnie's body lies still. His eyes are closed. I lean down and put my ear on his chest.

"Come on, Ronnie! Don't go away. Please . . ."

My own heart is beating so fast and loud I can't hear if his is beating. I try to calm myself but I can't.

I shake Ronnie's shoulders. "DON'T DIE," I shout at him. But he doesn't move.

Just then, while I'm trying to think where to go for help, I hear another voice in the house. It comes from downstairs. It's shouting my name.

"Dimple! Dimple!"

The voice is familiar, but I can't think straight. Can't make out who it is.

"Dimple!"

I hear footsteps running in the downstairs

hallway. I can hear breathing from whoever it is, even this far away. I can hear my own breathing too.

It's Ronnie's breathing I can't hear.

"Dimple!"

The voice is running up the steps now. Every footfall sounds like a shot. I can hear panic in the voice. *"Dimple!"*

I sit down on the bed next to Ronnie's body and look toward the open doorway. I still have one hand on his shoulder. Whoever's pounding up the stairway, they're going to see the truth of what I done in just a second. I hold my breath.

"Dimple!"

Sheila rounds the corner and runs into the room. I can tell she must of sprinted all the way from my house. She's sweating. Her face is red. I can even see veins pumping through her neck. Sheila *never* looks like this.

She comes straight over to me. But when she's only a step away, her eyes zero in on Ronnie's body. She screams. It's high and shrill. Not like in the movies. Not like when you're hurt real bad. Higher than that. It sounds like she's ripped her voice, torn it in two. Her scream comes from inside that tear, bloody and raw. It won't stop.

I let go of Ronnie and reach for Sheila. The red in her face drains away. What comes up in its place is a white the color of paste. The second I touch her, the scream stops. It sounds like somebody has scraped the needle off a record.

I grab hold of Sheila with both my hands. She slips through them, down toward the floor. I let go and grab again, lower on her body. I break her fall. She faints.

I straighten out her legs and lay her flat on the floor. Now I'm in a room with two bodies— Ronnie's and Sheila's, my two best friends. What if they're both dead, and I did it? I can feel my heart beating in my ears.

"Sheila?" I'm down on my hands and knees now, leaning over her face. "Sheila?"

All the blood has gone out of her face. In the movies, I've seen people slap somebody who's fainted. But I'm afraid to do this. I've done enough damage already.

I keep calling to her. "Sheila?"

After a second, I hear a distant answer, like it's coming from far away. "Huh? Wha . . . ?"

I lean my ear down close to her mouth. "Wake up, Sheila."

The weak voice comes again, but I don't feel or see any movement or breath from Sheila's lips.

Then the voice becomes suddenly loud and strong. "DIMPLE DORFMAN, YOU DAMN

137

FOOL. YOU TRIED TO KILL ME!"

I whip my head around and look at the bed. Ronnie's sitting up, white as a ghost.

My head feels dizzy. I taste rhubarb pie coming back into my mouth. My eyes go up, and I see the ceiling turn to the left. Slowly at first, and then faster. My eyes roll into darkness as I fall backward.

What are the odds of three people fainting in the same room within a few minutes of each other? The answer is: Pretty good, if one of 'em thinks he's just been shot, the second one runs into the room to find her best friend leaning over a dead body, and the third one sees a ghost. With a deal like that, you're gonna have bodies dropping left and right.

I'm the last one to come to.

Twice.

The first time I open my eyes I see Sheila's face and Ronnie's face about six inches away from me. I feel something cold on my forehead. One thought flashes into my head: I've died, gone to hell, and now Sheila and Ronnie are accusing me of killing 'em both. That does it. I faint again.

The second time I open my eyes there's Ivy June and Mrs. Fishback staring down at me. Then I *know* I'm in hell. I struggle to sit up and look around.

Ivy June is babbling about something. I hear my name, "Dimple," spoke over and over, about every other word, but I'm not listening. Mrs. Fishback is talking at the same time as Ivy June. She's using my name too. It's like "Dimple, Dimple, Dimple, Dimple."

I'm sitting on the floor next to the bed. I turn my head real slow to the left, then to the right. The room follows my sight, but it lags behind. I feel like I might faint some more, but I try to get focused. Ivy June and Mrs. Fishback are leaning in so close, I can't breathe.

"Give me some air," I mumble.

Mrs. Fishback backs off and goes, "What happened up here, Dimple Dorfman? What were the three of you doing up here anyway?"

I don't answer. I look around for the other two. At first I can't find 'em. Then I glance up.

Sheila and Ronnie are sitting on the bed side by side, looking like a couple grade-schoolers sent out to the hallway and told to keep quiet.

Ivy June's mother eases up. "You okay, Dimple?"

I nod at her.

"Ivy June thought she heard a gunshot, and I told her she was imagining things, but then she said she thought she heard screaming over here, and I told her she was imagining that, too, but then I saw the Delaneys' back door was wide open, and we came right over to investigate, and what do I find in here but Sheila and Ronnie sitting in a double bed together, and you passed out on the floor, and then Ivy June spots that gun laying there in the hallway, and I tell her not to touch it on account of fingerprints, and could you blame me if I thought there'd been another shooting over here, and maybe this one was on purpose? What do you young people have to say for yourselves? That's what I want to know."

Mrs. Fishback could take some grammar lessons from Ivy June. When she gets excited, her speech includes a serious shortage of periods.

Sheila speaks up. "It's very simple, Mrs. Fishback. Dimple and I came over here to visit Ronnie. After the trying day she's had, Dimple fainted. There was no gunshot. There was no screaming. Ivy June has an overactive imagination."

Ivy June cuts in. "What about *that*? Huh?" She points to the pistol laying in the doorway.

"That?" Ronnie says. He scoots out of the bed and slips past Ivy June and her mama. He picks up the gun and looks at it. "This here's a silly popgun. Just a toy."

Ronnie looks at me, and I feel the blood draining away from my head again. I know that gun weighs a whole lot more than his grip on it shows. I lean down and take some deep breaths.

"Let me see that," Ivy June demands.

But Sheila says, "No, Ronnie. You go put it away now. We wouldn't want to frighten Ivy June any more tonight."

Ronnie takes the cue and disappears down the hallway toward his parents' bedroom. I know where he's gonna put the gun. Once he gets into their bedroom, I can hear furniture scraping along the floor. He's hurrying to remake their bed and pull some duct tape off the chair. He comes back a couple minutes later with nothing in his hands.

Mrs. Fishback doesn't know whether to believe what we're telling her or not. "Are you sure you're okay, Dimple?"

"Yes, ma'am." I reserve that word for special occasions like this one.

I don't risk saying anything more. Sheila does all the talking for the three of us.

It takes about five minutes to sweet-talk Mrs. Fishback into believing she did her duty as a good neighbor, and that now it's time for her to take Ivy June home.

Ivy June's the one who keeps insisting, "But I

heard a gunshot, Mama, and I heard somebody scream. I swear it."

"Come along, Ivy June," Mrs. Fishback says.

Left alone, Ronnie and Sheila sit down on the floor next to me. I start crying. I can't help myself.

"Shhhh," Sheila goes, and takes my hand.

I pull away from her. I don't deserve no kindness. Not now. Not after what I done.

Ronnie doesn't speak. He just glares at me.

"Calm down, Dimple," Sheila says. "We're all done with fainting for tonight."

I look at Ronnie, and the tears come harder. I can't stop 'em. In the two days since Dale died, I haven't cried once. Now that I almost killed Ronnie, I cry and cry.

He keeps staring at me, but he still doesn't say a word.

Sheila grabs hold of my hand again. I keep trying to pull away, but she holds on for dear life. Finally, I ease up and let her have it. Once she hears what I done, she won't want to be my friend anymore, that's for sure.

I gotta tell her, but I can't stop crying.

I glance over at Ronnie. He's staring at me. I try to see if he's mad, but then I think how stupid that is. Of course he's mad. I just tied him up with duct tape. I just took a shot at him. I could of killed him. Fact is, I came to this house wanting to kill him. Why wouldn't he be mad?

I close my eyes. The river rises. Tears flood down my cheeks.

"Dimple, Dimple," Sheila sighs, making my name sound like a sad song. "It's over, Dimple."

Between sobs I say, "No, no."

"Yes, it is." Sheila strokes my hand. "It's all over now."

I shake my head. It hurts so much. I know this is *never* gonna be over. Nothing is ever gonna be over again.

"Stop it, Dimple."

This is Ronnie's voice speaking. I open my eyes.

"Stop crying, now. My folks could come home any minute, and we gotta talk."

I struggle to catch my breath. My sobs turn into hiccups, and then into gasps.

"Nothing happened over here tonight," Ronnie says. His voice sounds stern. He's taking charge. "I put the gun back. I—"

"NO," I shout at him. Now I can breathe good enough to talk, and I've got some things to say. "Something did happen over here tonight, Ronnie, and you know it. I shot you."

This confession of mine starts the waterworks

flowing again. It's like I opened a fire hydrant.

"You tried to shoot me, Dimple. That's for sure. But you missed. Do you see any hole?" Ronnie holds his arms out.

I shake my head. The tears keep seeping out.

Ronnie stands up and gets a pillow from off his bed.

"Look here, Dimple," he goes. "That's where the bullet went."

I try to see where he's pointing to, but everything runs together, blurry.

Ronnie hands the pillow over, takes my hand away from Sheila, and puts my finger right into the hole. "Feel that?"

I nod my head.

"That's where the bullet went."

I keep nodding.

"You missed me."

I pull my hands away from both Sheila and Ronnie. I clasp 'em together and wait for my breathing to get regular again. When it does, I speak.

"But I could of killed you, Ronnie." I keep my voice quiet and slow to where it won't crack.

He looks right into my eyes. "Yes, Dimple. You could of killed me."

"I wanted to kill you, Ronnie, that's right. But I

didn't want you to die. You gotta believe me about that. I wouldn't ever want you to die. Oh, I'm not making no sense."

"Yes, you are." Ronnie speaks slowly. "You needed to know what happened to Dale on that night. And I told you everything. Exactly like it happened."

I know now what Ronnie told me is the truth. Everything happened just the way he said it did.

I sit quiet, not speaking any more words. I try to breathe. I wipe away more tears. I sniffle.

Then I speak. "Ronnie?"

"What?"

"I'm sorry."

He stares into my eyes for a long time. His jaw is tight. Then he reaches over and takes my hand. "Me too, Dimple."

We sit there like that for a long time. Nobody speaks. Not me. Not Ronnie. Not Sheila.

Sheila takes the pillow off my lap and fingers around inside the bullet hole.

Finally, I take a big sniffle and say to Ronnie, "You sure you're not wounded?"

"Do you see any blood?"

I think he regrets the question the minute he asks it. He and I both jerk our heads toward the other side of the bed. But then neither of us looks.

"No," I say. "I don't see any blood."

He won't let go of my hand, and I don't want him to.

I can't say how long it is before we hear Mr. and Mrs. Delaney come in downstairs and shout calmly up at us. "Anybody home?"

It's what every neighbor says in Cuthbur.

Ronnie and Mr. Delaney walk Sheila and me back to my house. When we get there, Mama and Daddy don't look one bit worried. Just tired. Dead tired. I ask if Sheila can stay overnight, and they say sure.

Upstairs, Sheila and me crawl into my bed together. I ask her how she knew to come over to Ronnie's house. She says she waited a half hour for me to come out of my room. I didn't, so she came looking for me. When she saw the room was empty and the window was open, she remembered the plans I told her on the way to the cemetery and added two and two together. Then she told Mama and Daddy that me and her were going for a walk. She snuck out of the house and ran clear to Ronnie's. She says she heard the gunshot just as she was opening their back door. The rest of it you already know.

Out the window, in the moonlight, I can see the lights of some airplane in the far distance. I think about Dale and about heaven. But not in any story-book way. I'm no good at imagining angels and such. Just don't have that in me. All I can think about is where the airplane's going. Lying in my cool bed with Sheila's warm hand in mine, I think to myself, "I still got a twin engine inside me, but I'll be flying solo from now on."

"Dimple?" Sheila whispers.

I come back down to earth. "What?"

"I got something for you."

"What is it?"

"Wait until morning. You try to sleep now."

We lie there in silence for a long time. I reach my hand over on top of Sheila's arm. She scootches up closer. With her free hand, she strokes my hair.

We're in a pond, and we're swimming. It must be Aunt Nell and Uncle Lucky's pond, out behind their barn. Dale and me are five or six years old. I can see us clear as day. Mama calls us tadpoles—her "chubby little tadpoles"—because of how slick we take to the water.

We're still living in Alto Pass, before we moved into Cuthbur. Before we knew Ronnie. Before Sheila. Before Twin Protectors.

Dale and me are playing baptism, dunking each

other down in the name of the Father and of the Son and of the Holy Ghost. On the shore, Mama and Aunt Nell are spreading a picnic on a blanket. They're singing a song together, *My Love Is Waiting at the River,* harmonizing.

> *My love is waiting at the river.*
> *My love is waiting at the river.*
> *My love is waiting at the river.*
> *Waiting at the river for me-o.*

Dale and me keep baptizing each other, dipping under the water at the same time, hoping some of the magic of our sacred words will rub off.

> *Kiss me, my father and my mother.*
> *Kiss me, my sister and my brother.*
> *My love is waiting at the river.*
> *Waiting at the river for me-o.*

I wake up in the middle of the night. Some words from Mama's song are still floating in my brain. Sheila has rolled over the other way and is sound asleep.

I sit up and look out the window. The moon is bright.

Lying down again, I'd like to go back into my

dream, but I'm wide awake now. It was nice there. Just Dale and me together. Warm and wet in the pond.

I lie on my side with my back toward Sheila and face the window. I reach a hand under my pillow, the way I like to sleep. There's something under there—something small and hard. It takes me a few seconds to figure what it is. But once I know, I don't need to look.

I whisper into the night air. "Sheila, are you awake?"

"Uh?" she answers. She's still asleep.

"I found it. Thank you."

Sheila scootches her body into a more comfortable position.

"I wished to have it."

I lie there staring through the moonlit window, singing the dreamsong in my mind.

Kiss me, my father and my mother.

I finger the bullet underneath my pillow, rubbing its smooth surface and touching its hard steel.

Kiss me, my sister and my brother.

I feel a flood of tears rising, flowing toward me

around an unseen bend.

My love is waiting at the river.

I think about Sheila. And about Ronnie. I think about Twin Protectors. And, of course, I think about Dale.

Waiting at the river for me-o.

For the rest of my life, I'll think about him.
I let the flood come. It washes over me.